W9-BLA-200

DISNEY
TIM BURTON'S
THE NIGHTMARE BEFORE CHRISTMAS

LONG LIVE THE
PUMPKIN
QUEEN

FOR MY PARENTS
—S. E.

Copyright © 2022 Disney Enterprises, Inc. All rights reserved.

The movie, *Tim Burton's The Nightmare Before Christmas*, story and characters by Tim Burton. Copyright © 1993 Disney Enterprises, Inc.

Published by Disney Press, an imprint of Buena Vista Books, Inc.
No part of this book may be reproduced or transmitted in any form
or by any means, electronic or mechanical, including photocopying,
recording, or by any information storage and retrieval system,
without written permission from the publisher.

For information address
Disney Press, 1200 Grand Central Avenue,
Glendale, California 91201.
Printed in the United States of America

First Hardcover Edition, July 2022
1 3 5 7 9 10 8 6 4 2
FAC-004510-22140
Library of Congress Control Number: 2021949322
ISBN 978-1-368-06960-1

Designed by Soyoung Kim
Visit disneybooks.com

DISNEY

TIM BURTON'S
THE NIGHTMARE BEFORE CHRISTMAS

LONG LIVE THE
PUMPKIN
QUEEN

New York Times best-selling author
SHEA ERNSHAW

DISNEY PRESS
LOS ANGELES · NEW YORK

"I sense there's something in the wind, that feels like tragedy's at hand."

—Sally, *Tim Burton's*
The Nightmare Before Christmas

PROLOGUE

At the crisp, inky hour of midnight, Jack and I are married atop Spiral Hill in the Death's Door Cemetery. Wind stirs the bone-dry leaves, and Jack takes my soft rag doll hands in his—the coolness of his fingers calming the flutter rippling across my stitched seams.

The Mayor stands broad-chested before us, officiating the ceremony, his face alternating between corkscrew-eyed elation and pale, ghastly tears, while we speak our vows to each other in the grim custom of ancient wedding eulogies. The moon is a bloody red in the sky—a good omen—and a wilted oleander flower plucked from a patch of poison ivy at the far end of Halloween Town is tucked just behind my left ear—a custom that ensures a long, dreadful life.

I squeeze Jack's hands tighter. His black tuxedo tails sway in the cold night air while my dress, stitched from a scrap of black spinster lace—sewn myself the night before—billows like a ghost in the breeze. Cautiously, my gaze flicks to the crowd, where I can feel the cold, spiteful eyes of Dr. Finkelstein watching me from the front row, mouth quivering with fury now that I am finally escaping him, once and for all.

I am no longer your creation, I think, words knitted in my chest.

It seems unimaginable that barely a year ago, I feared I might spend my life trapped in Dr. Finkelstein's lab, fated to only ever watch Jack from afar—loving him but certain he would never know the ache I felt whenever he looked my way. But after Jack tried to steal Christmas from Sandy Claws, after he nearly died venturing to the human world to deliver our grim presents on Christmas Eve, with Zero leading his sleigh of skeleton reindeer—a plan I sensed was doomed from the start—I knew I couldn't spend my life without him.

I knew I wouldn't waste another night.

Under a dark snow-flecked sky, Jack and I walked out to the cemetery, his moon-hollow eyes sinking, *sinking*, into mine. And at last, after a lifetime of loving him from afar—my rag doll heart aching to know what it would feel like if he ever loved me back—we shared our first kiss on the crest of Spiral Hill.

The same place where we now stand . . . hand in hand.

The Mayor's face spins back around to reveal his wide, toothy grin, his black widow bow tie eerily shiny in the moonlight, and he announces Jack and me as *husband* and *wife*—voice bellowing over the crowd.

Jack leans forward, eyes damp at the edges, and presses his grave-cold mouth to mine—and my seams feel like they're going to fray and burst, like they can't contain this swollen, chest-widening feeling rupturing through me. A feeling so strange and unknown and peculiar that it makes me dizzy. Makes my head swim, my legs teeter.

Jack and I are married.

He wipes away the tear streaming down my cotton cheekbone to my chin and looks at me like his own chest is about to fracture. And for a moment, I'm certain they should just bury us both here, at the center of the graveyard. Married and died on the same day. Unable to contain the unspeakable, awful, wondrous emotion breaking against our eyelids.

The dreadful residents of Halloween Town applaud, tossing tiny dwarf spiders at our feet as we leave the cemetery, and the warmth in my chest feels like bats clamoring for a way out of my rib cage. Trying to break me apart.

I am now Sally Skellington.

The Pumpkin Queen.

And I'm certain I will never again be as happy as I am right now.

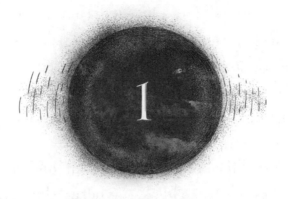

1

The evening skyline of Halloween Town is dotted with tiny pinholes of starlight, and across the town square, pumpkins glow a sinister copper orange. From Jack's house atop Skull Hill, the town looks different—draped in long, fingerlike shadows. The air smells different, too, like black licorice and raven wings and a little like pumpkin jam, nothing like the foul stench of sodium chloride and rubbing alcohol that permeates Dr. Finkelstein's lab, a place that was once my home—but also a prison.

The memory of it churns inside me, entwined with a feeling of stark relief that I will never again sleep inside that cold observatory. Never lie awake, alone in a narrow, moth-eaten bed, staring through a tiny window up at Jack's house in the distance, daydreaming of living within its walls someday.

It feels like a fairy tale from one of those happily-ever-after books where the princess storms the castle, slays a goblin-dragon, and takes over the kingdom for herself. Except I am not golden-haired or fine-boned. I have no bones at all.

I am a rag doll who married a skeleton king.

A rag doll who woke from the impossible daydream and found herself in her own heroine story—a tale whose ending hasn't yet been written; but instead, is only just beginning.

I leave the terrace overlooking the town and move back into the bedroom I now share with Jack, facing the tall, spiderweb-cracked mirror leaning against the slanted wall. I run my fingers through my hair, pulling it forward over my shoulder, the scarlet strands so coffin-straight that they could never be coiled or coiffed or pinned up with bat-bows. I press my palms against my patch-work dress, staring at my reflection in the glass: the crossed seams along my chest, the smile seams at the corners of my mouth, the places where Dr. Finkelstein stitched me together. Needle and thread and sinister midnight conjurings.

His creation, made in the dark, damp shadows of his lab.

A dead leaf pokes out from the seam along the inside of my left elbow—my stuffing coming loose—and I quickly push it back into place. My threads need to be re-stitched, leaves gathered and restuffed.

"You ready?" Jack asks. I turn, and he's standing in our bedroom doorway, holding a black velvet suitcase, the bottomless caverns of his eyes like graves I would happily tumble into, *down, down, down,* forever without end. A spider—a remnant of the wedding—skitters free from inside the suitcase and runs along the handle before it drops to the floor and falls into a crack. I had wanted to gather herbs from the garden—nightshade and bottle thorns—to take with us, just in case, but

Jack assured me that I wouldn't need such things on our honeymoon.

Potions and poisons aren't necessary outside of Halloween Town, he had said. There would be no need to poison or put anyone into a deathly sleep.

But it's hard for me to imagine a world where such things aren't needed.

I turn to smile at Jack–the seams on my cheeks stretching wide–and place my hand around the sturdy bones of his arm. *My husband.* The man I have loved for so long, at times it felt like it might crack me open. And together, we step out into the cool twilight of Halloween Town.

At the front gate of our home, guarded by two iron cats, spines raised, Jack pushes open the gate to face the waiting crowd–eager to catch a glimpse of the newly married king and queen– and he clears his throat. "My wife, Sally, and I are off on our honeymoon," he announces, grinning, showing all his corn-kernel teeth. "We'll be back tomorrow. If anything should happen, the Mayor will be in charge."

The Mayor, who stands beside one of the fanged metal cats, jerks his shoulders back at the same moment his face spins around, revealing the down-turned slope of his crooked mouth, and the deep worry in his small eyes. "Is that such a good idea, Jack?" he asks nervously. "Perhaps someone else should be in charge. Or maybe we should elect a committee. I'm not sure I can make decisions if an important matter were to arise. Or you could delay the honeymoon until after Halloween. It's only two weeks away," he reminds Jack. "Spring is a perfect time for a trip, or better yet, just skip the honeymoon altogether."

"You'll do great," Jack says, clapping the Mayor on the shoulder. The Mayor briefly reveals his smiling face, as if for a half second he believes he's up for the task, before his features swivel back around—lips a grim blue, worry rimming his terror-struck eyes.

But Jack is unfazed by the Mayor's apprehension—it's nothing new—and we make our way through the crowd, Jack shaking hands, accepting the congratulations of the townspeople who shuffle close, *too close*—crushing against us, hands reaching out—to see us off. But I slink back; the eyes of everyone on me feels like thorny stabs across my linen flesh, pulling me apart bit by bit. I'm not used to the attention, the whites of their eyes like hollowed-out ghosts, peering into my empty soul, judging, appraising. *Sally the rag doll, our Pumpkin Queen.* There is a festering thought inside me: perhaps they'll think I'm not worthy of the title. *A rag doll should never be queen.* A rag doll who should go back to the darkness of Dr. Finkelstein's lab, cold and solitary and alone.

They look at me like they're considering eating me whole.

Some of them probably would.

But then I catch a flash of white to my left, and Zero appears, pushing through the onlookers to nudge me in the elbow with his glowing jack-o'-lantern nose, and I stroke his ghostly white coat—the soft transparent feel of his fur, his sagging ears. The tightness in my chest calms, and he smiles his loose, open dog grin. To Zero, I'm no different than I was yesterday, before I married Jack, before I became queen.

With Zero hovering at my side, I follow Jack through the town center, ducking through the last of the crowd just as Lock, Shock, and Barrel—also known, woefully, as Boogie's Boys—shout, "We'll miss you, Pumpkin Queen!"

They've removed their trick-or-treat disguises, revealing their true faces—which are, somewhat perplexingly, identical to their masked facades—and they grin like the young children they are. Yet there is always a sly, crafty undertone hidden in their shimmering eyes that can't ever be trusted. It isn't their grins or their scheming giggles that sends a chill down the uneven stitching of my spine, however. It's the name they called me: *Pumpkin Queen.*

It's the first time I've heard it said out loud, and it rings in my ears all the way into the forest, to the Hinterlands, and the grove of seven trees.

"Are you sure it's safe?" I ask Jack, his face marred by shadows from the towering, spiny branches overhead. There was no wind on our walk through the woods, yet now the circle of trees shivers and vibrates, beckoning us closer. Jack taps a finger on the broad tree with a perfect heart, painted a buttery pink, carved at the center.

We are standing in the circular grove of seven trees that lead to seven holidays, where last year Jack slipped into Christmas Town and kidnapped Sandy Claws.

I've never been outside Halloween Town, never ventured beyond its borders, and I spin around now, slightly breathless, marveling at each strange carved tree. Each with its own peculiar doorway.

A green four-leaf clover adorns the tree for St. Patrick's Day; a red firework for the Fourth of July; a giant turkey marks the entrance to Thanksgiving; a pale painted egg for Easter; a Christmas tree with tiny baubles and lights leads to Christmas Town; and lastly, a grinning orange pumpkin for our home, Halloween Town.

After a pause, Jack steps toward the painted-heart doorway; a pink-and-white-striped box set near the trunk of the tree. "Of course," he answers, and I can hear the excitement in his voice. He's been to all the holidays, all the towns, except this one. He's been saving this tree for me. "I imagine

Valentine's Town will be more wondrous than all the rest. And now we'll see it together." He kisses the back of my hand, eyes tumbling into mine, then he tugs open the heart-shaped door nested in the trunk of the tree. A wind coils out from inside, soft and warm, smelling faintly of sugar cookies and wild roses.

I've never smelled anything so wondrous.

Still, nervously, I spin the bone-white wedding band on my finger, my eyes tracing the deadly nightshade vines engraved along the outer edge—a plant that has meant freedom for me, a way to escape Dr. Finkelstein each time I poisoned him with nightshade from the garden. *You are free now*, I remind myself, because although there is a buzzing of curiosity in my chest, there are also nervous crow wings flapping in my stomach.

But when I lift my gaze to Jack, his moonless eyes settle the restless crows, and the corners of my mouth tip upward. "I trust you," I say. Because I do, more than anything.

Jack nods, stepping his long, spidery legs through the opening into the tree, and pulls me in after him.

2

We fall headlong through the doorway, as if caught in a hallowed
breeze, until at last we spill out the
other side, landing in Valentine's Town—a place
wholly unfamiliar and strange. Quickly, I run my
fingers down my legs, checking my threads and
seams, to be sure none have split or tugged loose,
then I breathe in the gentle, sweet scent of sugared chocolate and roses in bloom. Surrounding
us stands a grove of trees—nearly identical to our
own: seven trees grown in a circle, one for each of

the seven holidays. Yet the forest overhead is thick with tall swaying branches, green leaves, and tiny white flowers stirring loose with each gust of wind. Nothing like the bony, leafless trees that populate the woods in Halloween Town.

Jack weaves his fingers through mine, grinning curiously, like he's just sprung from a shadow and frightened a ghost back into the dark—one of his favorite pastimes—and we follow the winding path out of the forest, away from the grove of seven trees. I run my fingertips along the dusty pink poppies and vibrant bloodred roses that line the path, and when we finally step free of the dense forest, I peer up at a cloudless sky, shimmering a soft airy pink.

"It's daylight here," I comment, surprised. "When we left Halloween Town, it was night."

"Every town has its own keeping of time, of sunrises and sunsets," Jack says, waving a hand toward the sky. "They're called time zones."

I squeeze his hand tighter, feeling briefly off-center, like my seams are tugging too tightly against my skin. Traveling from one town to another—one *time zone* to another—is strangely disorienting, and my head whirls and spins, as if I might tip over. "Where's their graveyard?" I ask as we follow the path through a rose-studded meadow, nearing the edge of the town. In Halloween Town, our graveyard rests on the outer border near the gate, where the howling voices of the dead can be heard echoing through the streets each night, and I expected to see one by now. If their cemetery is too far away, how will they ever be able to hear the tormented spirits of the dead?

"Not every holiday town has a graveyard," Jack explains, giving me a wink. "But look at all the hearts!" He points a bone-sharp finger toward an iron gate up ahead, hundreds of tiny hearts forged into the woven silvery metal. On either side of the gate sit two cherry blossom trees, the branches grown—or maybe trimmed—into the shape of a massive towering heart. It's an odd, unnatural sight, though certainly beautiful, and I wonder if here in Valentine's Town, all plants grow into such unusual shapes.

The trees sway and bob in the wind, releasing

their tiny blossoms into the air. "What do the hearts mean?" I ask.

"Apparently, Valentine's Day is a holiday that happens every February." Jack raises the bones above his eyes into his forehead. "And humans surprise one another with sweets and roses and poorly written love poems."

"Why?"

"Who knows!" Jack grins, tossing his gaze toward the town. "But isn't it wonderful?"

And truthfully, Valentine's Town is unexpectedly charming—in an odd, sideways sort of way. No sooty sky or charcoal buildings teetering in the distance. No rotted skulls or jack-o'-lanterns glowing sinisterly in the dark, no cackling ghouls or demons or grim reapers with hollowed-out eyes watching us from shadowed corners. In fact, there are no dark places at all. Instead, everything is bright and confectioner-sugar-shiny. The air has a pinked, dreamy quality, a subtly sweet tinge, like rosebuds newly bloomed in spring or the first lick of pumpkin-pie filling on a spoon.

It all seems twisted up and spit out wrong.

Yet my eyes sway from one hedged rosebush to another, my heart lilting in my chest in a way that makes me dizzy.

This place is something entirely unfamiliar, and undeniably delightful.

We pass through the heart-forged gate, and I can feel my seams relax just a little, my dead leaves settling in my chest, when the sky is blotted out above us. A mass of birds flock toward town, muting the candy-tinted sun.

But when I squint up at them, trying to make sense of their odd shape, I realize that they're not birds at all.

It's a flock of small baby-like creatures.

Five of them, fluttering above us: rosy-cheeked and plump-bellied, with tiny wooden bows and heart-shaped arrows strapped in sheaths at their small backs, white wings flapping.

"What are they?" I ask.

"No idea," Jack replies with a grin.

But they either don't notice us or don't care, and they continue their flight toward the shimmering mass of buildings ahead.

The worn dirt path soon becomes a cobblestone

street, taking us straight into the heart of Valentine's Town, and my eyes widen, not wanting to miss a single detail of the white chalky-stone homes that line the street–they look almost edible, with pink tiled roofs and heart-framed windows, and the stained glass reminds me of melted sugar, like you could press your tongue to it and it would surely taste sweet. I feel myself grinning as widely as Jack, urging him on, until at last we reach the town center, marked by a stone fountain with a carved cherry-cheeked baby at the top–identical to the flock of baby-creatures we saw flying overhead just outside of town. I lean against the edge of the fountain, peering down at the water, which glistens a pale candy pink–nothing like the swampy green fountain back in Halloween Town–my reflection staring back.

"Do you think we can drink it?" I ask, inching my hand closer to the water, certain it will taste like icing and marigold petals.

But before my fingertips can break the surface, a cool, velvety voice speaks behind us. "It's nice to see two lovers in town."

I straighten, and look up . . . and up . . . until at

last meeting the gaze of a woman who is a good foot taller than Jack. She is a tower, wearing a long chiffon gown with tiny white embroidered hearts stitched into the cream fabric of her skirt. Her strawberry red hair is coiled up into a honeycomb beehive, with a gold heart barrette clipped softly at her temple. "Visiting from elsewhere?" she asks vaguely, tapping her rosebud lips with a long painted fingernail. Her skin is a soft pinkish hue, as if she's been eating too many rose petals and it has begun to change the color of her flesh.

"I'm Jack Skellington," my husband announces, sticking out his hand. "The Pumpkin King, from Halloween Town. And this is my bride, Sally, the Pumpkin Queen."

"Yes, yes, good," she replies, ignoring his hand, as if she's uninterested in our names or the details of why we're here. She cares more about her own introduction. "I'm Queen Ruby Valentino, and this is my town." She trails a long elegant hand along one side of her dress in a flourished, wide-sweeping curtsy. I marvel at how poised she is, abloom with confidence. Even the features of her face are neat and organized, not a stray freckle out of place. She is a visage of what I've imagined perfect royal etiquette might look like, and I suddenly feel quite un-queenlike in her presence.

"It's our first visit to Valentine's Town," Jack replies cheerfully, shoulders back, undaunted by this woman's regal demeanor.

But Ruby's eyes suddenly snap away from us. "Gah!" she exclaims. "A bleeding heart! Paulo! Paulo, I told you to rip these out as soon as you see them."

A slim, high-waisted man appears as if he'd been crouched behind Ruby, awaiting any command she might thrust upon him. Wearing an apron, a straw sun hat, and long pale slacks, and clutching a pair of gardening shears in his dirt-stained hand, he wipes at his forehead quickly. "So sorry, Your Royal Highness, I must have missed this one."

Ruby gracefully bends toward the ground, despite her heavy gown and high heels, plucking a single flower with a bloodred center that had been growing up between the stone pavers that surround the fountain. She holds the flower up for us to see. "Can't have these bleeding hearts growing so near the fountain," she says, her mouth contorting into a disgusted little sneer.

I blink at the tiny, harmless-looking flower pinched between her fingers, summoning the question inside me as if I am a child afraid to speak. "Why's that?" My voice sounds much too small—meager and weak—not the words of a queen.

Ruby flicks her gaze to me, her sneer softening. "The cupids dip their arrows into the fountain, of course." She says it like I should already know this, and I gaze down into the water, light shimmering across the surface like little pink diamonds. "Our love potion bubbles up from a natural spring beneath the fountain." She raises her perfectly plucked eyebrows at me. "If a bleeding heart flower made its way into the fountain, then everyone who was struck by a cupid's arrow on Valentine's Day would suffer a *broken* heart instead of falling in love."

She tosses the flower onto the ground and crushes it with the toe of her lollipop-red high-heeled shoe. When she lifts her foot, Paulo—the man who stands with hands wringing beside her—quickly skitters forward and retrieves the flattened flower from the ground. "I'll burn it immediately," he says, then scurries off.

Ruby smiles softly, pleased, then tilts her gaze back at Jack and me. "Do you have a place to stay?"

Jack clears his throat. "Not yet."

"Follow me," she says with a flourish, her voice now a singsong, a collection of musical notes as though a bird is resting at the back of her throat, and she leads us away from the fountain. We pass a café, where the scent of rising dough fills the air, and a dentist's office with a painted window that reads HALF-PRICE CAVITY REPAIR. Then in smaller print: FREE LOLLIPOP WITH EACH TOOTH REMOVAL. The people who stroll past us, doughy-eyed and full cheeked, always seem to be in pairs—arms woven together, secret words whispered into each other's ears. They sit side by side on café patios, faces nestled together, kisses planted on bare necks. And many of them have tulips pinned at their lapels or tucked neatly into shirt pockets, while others have wildflowers braided into their hair.

Love is imbued into every seam and stitch of this town. It's inescapable. And I feel the dead leaves in my chest swelling and swimming at the sight of it all.

Another block more, and Ruby stops in front of a brick building. Above us, the swaying wooden sign reads LOVEBIRD INN.

"Wait here," she says, winking, then disappears into the narrow doorway. Moments later, she reappears clutching a silver key. "You'll be staying in one of the cottages around back; they're perfectly quaint and well-appointed. You should be quite happy there."

Jack smiles, taking the key from her. "Splendid! Thank you."

Ruby resecures a stray pin that has come loose from her wavy cherry-red hair just as her eyes flash upward. "Slow down!" she shouts.

Above us, a clot of the winged babies flutter over the town, before disappearing into the distance.

Ruby lets out an irritated sigh. "The cupids are so unruly this time of year, restless little trouble-makers." She gives me a look, as if I should have an idea of what she's talking about. "They grow bored with nothing to do, just waiting for

February–for Valentine's Day–so they fly in packs, stirring up all sorts of mischief." She blows out a quick breath through her nostrils. "Cupids can only be trusted on Valentine's Day. The rest of the year they're an awful nuisance."

Ruby peers at me with her soft chocolate eyes, gaze roving from my feet to the top of my head, like she's surveying my appearance for the first time. She tilts her head and plants a delicate hand on her hips. "Your hair is a little dull for a queen," she remarks. "My stylist could weave in a few curls, maybe a highlight or two, have you looking a little more"–she taps a fingernail against her bottom lip–"well, like me." A smile sparks in her clear, dewy eyes. "I'd be happy to make an appointment for you while you're here."

I shake my head quickly, not liking the prying feel of her eyes on me, the sharp appraising look. "I don't think–" I start picking at the loose thread on my left wrist, making it worse. "No–thank you."

She shrugs, turning her attention up the street, where two lovers are entangled in the doorway of a chocolate shop–a tall, lean dark-haired man reciting words to a man with curly blond hair and freckles, a poem that it seems he's written himself, the words scribbled onto a pink piece of paper he holds in his palm.

Ruby sighs softly, as if caught in the sweetness of the moment—the tenderness between two people madly, deliriously in love. She wipes at her eye, as if a tear is about to fall, then she turns to look back at Jack and me. "Say," she begins, her eyelashes flitting, "you two wouldn't happen to know someone named William Shakespeare?"

Jack lifts the bones above his hollow eyes. "Sorry, no."

Ruby lets out a long, troubled sigh, puckering her full painted lips. "He writes the most beautiful sonnets, and I'm certain he is my one true love, but I'm having a terrible time finding him."

Jack pauses, and we share a look. There are many books in Jack's library written by William Shakespeare—beautiful, often tragic stories—but they are rather old, and I'm certain William Shakespeare is good and dead, quite some time ago now. But I give Jack a quick shake of my head, not wanting to break Ruby's heart by telling her as much.

"If we come across him," Jack adds with a gentle smile, "we'll certainly send him your way."

"Thank you." Ruby's mouth curves upward, even while her eyes betray a glimmer of sadness. "I hope you both enjoy your stay with us. It should be a lovely day to stroll the city. Make sure you stop at Romeo's Delicatessen. They make the most divine caramel teardrops you've ever had in your life."

I have no idea what a caramel teardrop is, but I'm certain Romeo's Delicatessen is named after Romeo from Shakespeare's play *Romeo and Juliet*–a reminder of the man who Ruby has never met but loves anyway.

She gives us a quick curtsy before turning away and sauntering down the cobblestone street. I watch her a moment as she stops to speak to shop owners and townspeople, shaking hands–a queenly silhouette against the sugared, heart-carved backdrop of her town.

I'm certain I don't cast quite as striking a queenly figure in Halloween Town.

I'm all rounded edges and dead leaves spilling out from loosened seams. I am nothing like her.

A sharp blade of doubt edges into my thoughts. *Maybe I am more unprepared for this role than I realized.*

But Jack folds his hand over mine, and the look of excitement in his eyes forces my own stirring thoughts to retreat. We find the path that winds around Lovebird Inn, to where a dozen small cottages sit like kisses nestled between the tall grass and rustling white pine trees. Jack slides the key into the lock of cottage number five, set on the far left of the others.

"Who else comes to stay here?" I ask curiously.

"Anyone, I suppose," he says. "Those from other holidays who pass through the doorways and want a weekend away, a vacation."

We push into the little cottage and are met with the scent of vanilla-jasmine candles and rose petals scattered along the wood floor. Jack places our suitcase beside the bed.

"Why does no one come to Halloween Town to visit?" I ask, walking to the lace curtain and pulling it back to look out on Valentine's Town.

"We don't have an inn—" Jack's eyes lift, his peculiar smile curling upward. "But perhaps we should. Tourism might be good for the town."

I let the curtain fall back into place, and Jack crosses the room, taking my hands in his. "There's so much to see," he says at last, kissing my palm. "And not a moment to waste."

With our suitcase now deposited into our cottage, we venture back out into Valentine's Town.

The day is a whirl of chocolate confections dipped in hazelnuts and caramelized brown sugar, raspberries coated in white chocolate, and chalky little hearts with words stamped onto their surface: *Love Bug, Sweet Pea, XOXO.* We eat them by the handful, our cheeks flushed from the sugar, chests thumping wildly. We even pass a factory where the hearts are made, stacks of little pink boxes lined up in the windows, surely to be delivered to the human world once Valentine's Day arrives.

"Even the air smells sweet," I say, popping a cherry truffle into my mouth as we wander the cobbled streets, feeling the chocolate break apart on my tongue.

Jack takes my hand and twirls me in a circle. "I knew you would love it here."

I think how heavenly it must be to nibble on tiny cakes and swirled caramels and plum ginger puffs all day. Tea with lemon petit fours in the afternoon; after-dinner mint truffles with butterscotch coffee in the evening. My mind swims with the notion of it. The easy, sugar-induced lull that would follow me into candy-tinted dreams each night. Life here, in Valentine's Town, would surely be simple and uncomplicated.

Outside a small patisserie—the window display filled with trays of butter cookies—a squat woman is ordering a box of meringues from the gray-mustached man in the doorway, and beside her is a lace-trimmed pram, filled with three wailing babies. They all have a twirl of dark hair atop their otherwise bald heads, skin the color of figs just like the woman, with lips stained a bright pink, and a dusting of powdered sugar along their fingertips and white bibs.

I bend down and touch the chubby hand of one of the crying infants, and it immediately grabs my pointed finger and squeezes, giggling, showing its gummy, toothless mouth. The other two infants stop crying and peer up at me with their moon-saucer eyes—all three gazing at me as if they were looking at the night sky in wonder.

"Well done," the squat woman remarks, nodding down at me. "They usually don't quiet for anything but sweets. But they certainly like you."

She places her box of cookies atop the little awning of the pram.

"Are they cupids?" I ask, curious why these babies are tucked into a pram, while we've seen others flying through town with tiny bows and arrows.

"They will be, once they grow their wings," she answers, bending down to straighten the white ruffle tunic on the third baby in the back. "Have a sweet day," she says to me, smiling, before starting to push the pram away. The baby releases my finger and begins making a fussing sound, followed by a full wail. But the woman keeps pushing them up the cobbled street, humming to the infants in a gentle, sugary singsong.

I wonder if someday Jack and I will have our own pram filled with tiny skeletons and rag dolls.

The scuttle of little feet through the house. Skeleton boys tumbling down the spiral stairs; little rag doll girls with their threads coming loose, always needing their fingers and toes stitched back together. A perfectly grim little family.

Jack plucks a single lavender rose growing beside the patisserie, then holds it out to me. "For the queen of Halloween Town," he says with a goofy little tip of his head, as if he likes the sound of it. *Queen.* But the word echoes along the walls of my fabric insides, making me shiver. Still, I take the flower from him and bring it to my nose—all soft petals and a silky springtime scent.

Jack weaves his fingers back through mine and whisks me up the street, away from the main center of town, and down a winding path through a thicket of stargazer flowers that opens up to a wide river.

Four small wooden boats sit tied to the shore, and Jack climbs into the bow of one with a lavender heart painted on the side, then takes hold of an oar.

"I don't think we should," I say. "We don't know who they belong to."

"We'll only borrow it," he replies with a wink, and I can't help smiling back. He takes my hand and helps me into the teetering little boat.

We push off from shore, and I dip my hand down into the water, but the surface is thick like mud. "What is it?" I ask.

Jack runs a finger along the top, then brings it to his mouth. "Chocolate." He sinks his hand in again, then leans forward to place a dollop of warm melted chocolate on the end of my nose. I laugh, wiping it clean, then scoop up a handful of the chocolate river and lob it in his direction. He ducks just in time, barely missing it and grinning wildly, but he doesn't see the next wad of chocolate I launch toward him, and it splats right across his bone-white face. A deep, rolling belly laugh rises inside me, and I buckle forward, giggling so hard I fear I might split one of my seams. Jack is still laughing when I climb over the narrow bench seat separating us and kiss him square on the lips, tasting the sugary sweetness of dark chocolate.

"Thank you for bringing me here," I whisper against his mouth.

He smiles. "We can spend our lives exploring the other holidays, together, as king and queen." He kisses me again, his hand tracing the seam along my right cheekbone.

But the word catches in my chest again: *queen.* Like a thorn pricking at my linen flesh, digging in deeper, burrowing. I can't seem to shake it.

"I'm still not used to it," I admit softly, leaning back against the side of the boat.

"What?" Jack asks.

"Being called a queen."

Jack rests the oars on the edge of the boat and leans forward, letting the current pull us through the canals of Valentine's Town, along the boardwalk, lined with cafés and chocolate shops and even a greeting card store with handmade paper cards fluttering in the window. "Halloween Town has never had a queen before," he says, tracing the stitching along my palm with his bony finger. "You are the first." His dark moonless eyes stare into mine, rooting me to him, and I feel a comfort in his gaze I've never known in anything else. "You are now the queen of all of Halloween."

I bite the side of my cheek, lowering my chin. "What if I don't know how to be queen? What if I do it all wrong?" I peer at Jack through my eyelashes, afraid to meet his gaze dead-on. "Ruby Valentino was so charming and flawless and queenlike, and I don't know if I can be like that."

Jack reveals a half smirk, glancing at me through his hooded eyes. "You're not the queen of Valentine's Town. . . . You are the queen of Halloween Town." He lifts his chin and smiles fully. "And since you are the very first queen, you get to decide how you want to rule." He kisses my palm, lingering there, before lifting his eyes to mine again. "You are the Pumpkin Queen, Sally. You can do whatever you want."

I nod, wanting to believe him. Needing to. Because the doubt churning in my stomach feels like tomb beetles tunneling through a corpse in the graveyard. Breaking me apart.

He shifts closer, the boat rocking beneath us, and he kisses me again, the coolness of his lips soothing my rumbling thoughts for the tiniest of moments. He kisses me deeper, wrapping his palm around my back, along the seam of my spine, and

I feel anchored to him—my fabric flesh bound to the cold of his skeleton bones. His fingers find my neck, my jaw, and I feel myself breaking, melting, sinking beneath his touch. Like he will never let me go. Like we could stay this way forever, drifting down a chocolate river.

I tell myself to forget who I'm *supposed* to be.

Because right now I am simply a rag doll in a boat with a skeleton whom I love. Madly. Feverishly. Floating through a town where my title doesn't matter. *Queen, queen, queen.* Where no one knows who I am.

At last, Jack lifts his mouth from mine, and little sparks blink behind my threaded eyelashes. I want to pull him back to me, tell him not to let me go, but the boat has shifted, slowed against a clot of chocolate truffles along the bank, and Jack lifts the oars, steering us back into the center of the river, where the chocolate current takes us beyond the edge of town, winding into a small rose-hued forest.

I sink back against the bow of the boat, letting my arm drape over the side, watching Jack row with each perfect stroke of his arms, a bead of sweat glinting on his forehead. I tilt my eyes back and stare up at the perfectly blue sky, wanting to lose myself in a daydream, in the foolish idea that we could stay here in Valentine's Town forever.

Two cupids flutter past overhead, a thin line of heart glitter trailing down behind them.

I like it here, in the quiet of this strange forest, where pink tulips grow wild beneath the canopy of trees, and hearts have been carved into the white elms with names etched into the bark.

Jack + Sally. 4ever.

We watch the cotton-candy-pink sunset fade beyond the trees outside town, sipping glasses of muddled tulip wine, then collapse onto the feathery-soft bed inside the cottage, giggling, hands entwined, and I'm certain no moment could ever be as perfect as this. The swimming in my chest, Jack reciting nonsense poems, then laughing to himself. I want this to last forever. I want it to always be just Jack and me, side by side, until the end of time.

But when I finally drift off to sleep, my dreams are fitful and strange.

I dream of Halloween Town pulled into a nameless darkness. I wander the streets alone, struggling to make sense of each building, calling out to Jack, searching for him—in the shadowed-dark of our home, in Dr. Finkelstein's lab, even on Spiral Hill where we shared our first kiss. I grow desperate, fear edging along my seams. I stand in the center of town, and I scream.

The echo of it rattles in my ears, my chest, and I bolt awake—the blankets pulled up to my throat, Jack sound asleep beside me.

I relax my fingers against the pale pink blankets—embroidered with little hearts—and turn onto my side, peering at the small square window. A dim pastel light is breaking through the trees, slanting into our little cottage.

It's already morning.

But my dream of Halloween Town—of the darkness that slunk along dusty corners, a terror building in my throat—lingers inside me. Unshakable.

Jack stirs beside me, reaching out a hand to

stroke his fingers through my hair. "Good morning, wife," he says softly.

I turn to meet his eyes, the coldness rimmed
around their dark center, familiar in a way I don't
think I will ever tire of. "Good morning, husband,"
I echo.

He pulls me closer and we stay this way for a
time, his breath against my ear, a moment I don't
dare shatter with words–by telling him of the
dream, of the nerves bouncing along my stitched
ribs. But soon the birds begin to chatter from the
trees, and the sounds of Valentine's Town waking
echo through the streets, reaching us in the quiet
of the cottage.

Our honeymoon is over.

After a breakfast of butterscotch pancakes
with caramel syrup, Jack carries our suitcase
through the cottage door, and we make our way
beyond the edge of Valentine's Town, back to
the grove of seven trees. I pause and glance over
my shoulder, the scent of sugar cookies dipped in
chocolate hanging in the air. I still hold the lavender rose Jack picked for me yesterday, but the
farther we walk from Valentine's Town, the more

the petals begin to wilt, turning dry in my hand. It won't last. By the time we return to Halloween Town, it will surely be dead.

A flower that is only meant for this world.

"Ready to go home?" Jack says with a grin once we've entered the circle of trees.

"I wish we could stay a little longer," I admit.

He pulls open the door with the orange pumpkin etched into it. "Halloween is only two weeks away," he reminds me. "We need to get back."

I nod, tilting my eyes up to the branches one last time, where the wind has shaken loose molecule-sized flowers and set them free on the warm air.

"But we'll return," he assures, holding out his hand for me to take.

I had been nervous about leaving Halloween Town, but now, only a day later, I find I'm not ready to go back.

Still, I take Jack's hand, and we step through the small doorway, a whirl of tiny pumpkins spinning past my vision, and in an instant, we're whisked back to Halloween Town.

3

"They're back!" the Vampire Prince exclaims.

"How many witches were there?" the Witch Sisters ask in unison, scuttling up to Jack and me as soon as we enter the town square. "Were they as hideous as us?"

"Were there any walking dead?" Mummy Boy mumbles between his thick layers of cotton, his single eyeball blinking.

"I bet there were red-eyed demons, like me," the

Winged Demon remarks, nodding with certainty.

But Corpse Kid shakes his head. "No way. I bet there were girl demons."

I force a smile as the town residents surround us—shouting their questions, wanting us to describe Valentine's Town in detail. My head pulses, and I crave the dark quiet of our home atop Skull Hill, but Jack grins at the crowd.

"We did see a few winged babies," he says with a wink, patting Corpse Kid on his pale bald head.

"Did they have fangs?" the Winged Demon asks.

"Or poisonous horns?" Corpse Kid suggests.

But Jack shakes his head. "They're called cupids, and they make people fall in love."

At once, the faces in the crowd pucker in disgust. "Gross!" the Winged Demon says, sticking out his forked tongue.

"But how many ghouls do they have?" Mummy Boy asks now. "How many pumpkins and graveyards and deathly crawly things?"

Jack lets out a little chuckle, lifting his palms in the air. "All in good time," he assures them. "I will tell you everything we've seen. But for now, let us get resettled."

Still, they clamor around us. "Pumpkin Queen!" someone calls over the others. I turn and there is a sudden flash of a camera. It's the Clown with the Tear-Away Face, wheeling close on his unicycle, holding a camera to his yellow eyes and snapping another photo of Jack and me. "It's for the front cover of tomorrow's *Ghosts & Ghouls* newspaper," he shouts to us, his unicycle tire briefly lodging itself in a street crack before he wobbles free. "Everyone wants to hear about the royal couple's trip."

Jack grins at the Clown and exclaims, "Wonderful!"

But I feel wholly overwhelmed. Too many hands reach out for us, touching the fabric of my dress, as if I'm someone new and unfamiliar they've never seen before. As if I'm not the same person I was before I married Jack. Before yesterday. They push one another aside, trying to get closer—to see me better. And I hate the way it makes me feel. *Examined, scrutinized.* As though

I am some nighttime creature they have caught in their net and are about to dissect.

I push my way behind Jack as we finally approach the gate to Skull Hill, the procession following close behind. "Jack!" the Mayor shouts, waiting for us at the metal gate, tapping nervously at the orange ribbon on his coat pocket that reads MAYOR, lest anyone should forget. "We have many things we must discuss. Halloween is only two weeks away."

"Yes, of course!" Jack replies. "Come inside!"

I wince, my stomach plummeting. I want nothing more than to shut the door of our home, sink into the quiet, and be alone with Jack. But the Mayor waddles in behind us, his cone-shaped head barely squeezing through the doorway, and several others bustle in behind him, including the Witch Sisters—Helgamine and Zeldaborn—and the Vampire Prince.

"Sally—I mean . . . Queen," the Mayor corrects himself, clearing his throat. "The Witch Sisters and the Vampire Prince have many things to show you. There isn't much time."

"For what?" I ask, backing away from the Mayor,

hoping I can slip through one of the shadowy doorways and escape his frenzied, swivel-eyed gaze.

"As queen, you will be organizing the All Hallows' Eve party in the cemetery this year. It's quite an honor. Plus, there are the new curtain swatches to be decided on. You can't possibly live in this house without redecorating."

"And your new gown!" Helgamine and Zeldaborn say in unison.

I swallow down the scrabbling, thorny ache forming in my throat and feel for the seam on my wrist, picking at the thread. Tugging at it. Worrying it loose. "I don't need a new gown."

The Mayor's face jerks around quickly, revealing his sharp pointed teeth and a deep, grisly frown. "Nonsense. You're the Pumpkin Queen now. You can't keep wearing that tattered old thing." He nods at my patchwork dress, the one I have re-stitched so many times that I'm certain none of the fabric patches are the originals, the black-as-night thread barely keeping it together.

"Must anything change at all?" I ask, my voice too thin, like air slipping through cracks on a

winter night, like I'm unsure of my own words. "I
don't think the house needs new curtains, either."

The Vampire Prince lowers his black umbrella—
his shield from the cruel sunlight when he's
outdoors—and folds it into a narrow point before
walking to the front window, touching the old
black curtains with his thin fingertips, and making a *tsk–tsk* sound. Like he's never seen anything
quite so horrid in his long, *long* life.

"Maybe we could at least wait until tomorrow," I suggest, backing away toward the spiral
stairs. "Start in the morning." I don't want a new
dress, new curtains, or to make plans for a party. I
just want to be alone with Jack for a little longer,
pretend we're back in Valentine's Town, drifting
lazily down the chocolate river, his eyes settled
on mine, making me feel safe, making me feel at
home, with none of the obligations waiting for us
here.

But the Mayor waves a hand at me. "No, no,
there's no time to waste." And before I can protest further, he has turned his attention to Jack,
who has already started down the hall toward

his library, mumbling to himself as he thumbs through the scrolls of diagrams and sketches for the fast-approaching Halloween holiday. Already lost in his work.

Alone with the Witch Sisters and the Vampire Prince, I think I can make my escape—slink away into the kitchen, or even a closet, where I will hide and wait for them all to leave. For hours or days if I must. A queen hiding in her own home. But Helgamine—the taller of the two sisters—grabs my wrist with her sharp fingertips, pinching my fabric tightly, then leads me up the stairwell to the bedroom Jack and I share.

I let out a little squeak, but I don't fight her.

The sun dips below the horizon, giving way to night, and in the bedroom, the fireplace crackles and spits out sparks onto the rug, while the stone gargoyles scowl down at us from the ceiling, and I feel at once like a prisoner in my own home. Confined by the sisters and the Vampire Prince, blocking the stairs.

"Stand up straight," Zeldaborn instructs, even though she is a good foot shorter than me, her wavy black hair sticking out from beneath her pointed hat like an overgrown blackberry bush. "A queen should certainly have better posture than yours." She jabs me in the ribs with her long index finger, her nail like a metal spike.

"And better hair," Helgamine chimes in, taking a strand of my straight rose-red hair between her fingers and making a disappointed grunting sound. Helgamine's own ghost-white hair is just as unruly as her sister's. "My broomstick is silkier than this."

They both cackle, buckling over at their shared joke. The Witch Sisters were surely young and wartless once, but now they are bent at the shoulders, wiry and hollow-eyed like dusty relics. Their joints crack and pop as they scuttle around me, and their breath is like a bog. Yet they have no problem pointing out my apparent flaws, as if I am a sad, lost cause.

Before I married Jack, Helgamine and Zeldaborn never seemed to notice me—I was as unimportant to them as a scarab beetle crushed beneath their shiny black shoes. But now, between grumbles of annoyance and snickering laughter, they drape black chiffon across my torso, then pin it to my patchwork dress, as if I am . . . well, a rag doll. Accustomed to the pricks of needle points.

They stand back to admire their work before re-pinning and fussing and adjusting seams.

The Vampire Prince ignores their wheezing laughs, and juts out his long gray chin as he steps forward to place an oversized black feathered hat atop my head. But when I catch my reflection in the slender mirror beside the bedroom closet, I see that it's not a hat at all—it's a crown.

The Vampire Prince tilts it a little to the left, then forward, so that it's slumped partly over my eyelashes.

"Hmmm, we *vant* you to *veel* perfectly queenly," he says, blinking his milk-white eyes at me.

I grimace at the word—always the same word, *queen*—as I push the crown higher onto my head, away from my eyes. *But I feel like an imposter.* I look like one, too.

Zeldaborn and Helgamine cease their laughing to appraise the crown. "If you don't like the crow feathers," Zeldaborn says, giving me a curious look, "I saw a raven in the street this morning, newly dead. It would look lovely with your pale complexion."

I scratch at the side of the crown, where my hair is tugging against the feathers. "Must I wear a crown at all?"

The Vampire Prince gasps, then clutches a hand to his mouth, as if I have personally offended him.

"Jack doesn't wear a crown," I point out.

Helgamine and Zeldaborn exchange quick looks, their laughter gone, their raised warts gleaming in the moonlight through the window.

The Vampire Prince paces in front of me, arms crossed, his sharp black hairline drawing down. "Crowns are all the fashion for queens these days."

"How would you know what the latest fashions are?" I ask, a rotting discomfort growing inside me, an itch at the base of my neck—like the walls are shrinking, tipping closer; and soon they will crush me into a heap of chiffon and crow wings. "None of you have ever been outside Halloween Town," I continue, my voice rising, sounding stronger now. But the room only grows smaller, the seams along my chest tightening, until it feels impossible to suck in a breath. "You've never even met a real queen before."

I have . . . but I don't tell them this—about my meeting with Ruby Valentino—because I have no interest in wearing cherry-red high heels and a bouffant glittery gown that sweeps around me like a broom wherever I walk. Surely such a gown would only gather up beetles and spiders in its hemline, a place for insects to nest and make their home. "I don't need any of this," I say instead, my head dizzy, my throat dry, like I've swallowed down spoonfuls of dust.

Zeldaborn's expression curdles. Helgamine's mouth falls open.

With the chiffon fabric still pinned across my patchwork dress, and a crow-feather crown tipping to one side of my head, I start to back away from them—toward the doorway—feeling trapped like a pigeon in an attic, wings useless, eyes darting for a way free. The trio stare back at me, eyes blinking, but before they can argue that this is for my own good, I slip out into the hall and scramble down the staircase, tripping on the layers of chiffon.

At the end of the hall, I duck into Jack's library, breathing deeply.

Jack and the Mayor are hunched over the unrolled sketches and blueprints spread out on the lopsided wood table, talking quickly, heads close together, while Jack uses a squid-ink pen to makes notes in the margins. "Perhaps we should use twice as many spiders this year," Jack is saying. "Tuck them into the corners of every bedroom."

The Mayor nods. "Cobwebs are always a success," he replies, tapping a finger against the table. "And remember, production is down with candy corn this year, so we'll need to find an alternative."

Jack straightens. "Is the swamp still running low on sugared wax?"

"Afraid so. But we have an idea for making candies shaped like bat heads."

Jack rubs anxiously at his forehead, bone against bone. "Do we have enough black tar for that?"

"I'll check with Cyclops, but last week he assured me that the tar pits were as deep as ever."

"Good," Jack says, releasing his hand. "Now, about the Wolfman, I heard he has a sore throat and isn't sure if he'll be able to howl at the moon this year. Is this true?"

The Mayor starts to speak, but I step into the room, cutting him off. "Jack," I say softly. "I need to speak with you."

He turns and smiles when he sees me, eyes lighting up.

"I—" I step farther into the room, into the lamplight. "I don't really feel like myself in all this." I lift the edges of the black chiffon gown for him to see, the layers like a lace cake, or cobwebs stretched thin, the crow-feather crown now slumped to one side, slipping down my too-straight hair.

Jack raises the bones above his eyes, mouth puckering to one side. "Hmm," he muses, crossing the library to touch a length of the fabric stretched and pinned across my shoulder. "It does seem a little strange. A little too"—he considers the right word—"formal? Perhaps a different fabric?"

I swallow and shake my head. "Jack, I don't think—"

But the Mayor cuts me off. "They're doing the best they can with the fabric they have, Jack." The Mayor's face has spun around again, all jagged teeth and worried eyes. "Halloween and a queen all in less than a month, it's a lot for the town to organize. We're stretched thin as it is."

Jack nods. "Yes, of course, I know I'm asking a lot of everyone."

"It's not the fabric—" I start.

But Jack takes my hand in his. "I want you to have anything you need to feel like a queen," he says. "A new dress, new shoes, whatever you want. Perhaps you can suggest to them a different style. Or a crown that's a little less . . ." He taps a finger to his chin.

"I don't want *any* of these things," I interject, shaking my head. "I don't want a crown at all."

He tilts his gaze, like he's finally starting to understand. To see the worry dampening my eyes.

"Jack, please!" the Mayor says from the table. "You've already been gone for your honeymoon!

We don't have time to argue over dress fabrics."

"Yes, yes," Jack replies, nodding back at the Mayor; then he turns his focus to me, taking my hands in his. "We'll discuss it tonight," he says, winking at me. "I only want you to be happy." He says it softly, so only I can hear, then he kisses my palm, soft and sweet.

But all too quickly, he turns back to the Mayor, resuming their conversation about how many pumpkins should be carved and how many beetle-wax candles to place in each.

I tuck my mouth to one side, the unease still writhing inside me, and I slip out into the hall, where the Witch Sisters and the Vampire Prince are coming down the stairs. "Pumpkin Queen!" they call in a chirpy singsong. "Let us show you the fish leather shoes we've prepared for you. The heel is impossibly tall and terribly uncomfortable; we think you'll love it."

I don't wait for them to reach the bottom of the stairs.

I don't bother protesting.

Instead, I dash past them and yank open the front door, ducking out into the dim evening light.

4

I have to get away from Halloween Town.
Away from everyone.
My mind hisses with overcrowded thoughts, like poison bubbling over—left to simmer too long on a crackling fire. I wanted this, didn't I? To marry Jack.

But I never truly wanted to be *queen*. I was happy to remain a rag doll—imperfect, broken in places. Hair straight as a board and dry as bone. A girl unchanged.

But that's not true, either. I was never content in my life before Jack. Never satisfied to remain trapped in Dr. Finkelstein's lab. Never liked the idea of being *built*, molded, sewn together by a mad scientist in a cold, damp lab, on a dark, rain-drenched night.

I wanted something else, something more than the life I was given.

But now I'm queen and it feels like there are pieces missing between my two lives—seams not properly folded together. Jagged and knotted.

Parts of myself I don't quite understand.

Night lies heavy over Halloween Town, and I make my way quickly along the outer edge of town, through long sinister shadows, until I reach the cemetery. Zero appears in the doorway of his small tombstone doghouse, eyes black as night, ears raised. He zips after me—nose glowing golden orange in the dark—and together we cross over the narrow stone bridge, leaving Halloween Town behind, and pass into the starless gloom of the forest.

I need the quiet of the woods. The cool night

air to fold itself over me and make me feel safe, sheltered, invisible. Only a rag doll, nothing more.

Dr. Finkelstein used to call me a foolish dreamer. He said I spent too much time in the garden or peering up at the night stars. *A girl who lives inside her own head.*

I knew that my life would change when I married Jack—that it wouldn't be a simple elf-princess and her frog-prince kind of fairy tale. But I hadn't imagined *this*. That I would finally be free of Dr. Finkelstein but still not feel like myself. A girl whose life had always been decided for her and would discover the same dark prison walls once she became queen. And I wonder: do other queens and princesses and duchesses feel as I do? In other realms, other times? Have they peered at their reflections in ponds and warm bathwater and magic mirrors and wondered who they've become? How they lost the girl they once were? Certain that they are more than a puppet, strings yanked this way and that, pulling them apart? Does Ruby Valentino catch sight of herself in a shop window from time to time and not recognize the woman staring back?

"You still think I'm the same girl, don't you, Zero?" I ask as we make our way deeper into the woods, under the cover of starlight and swaying bare branches.

Zero's nose glows brighter, and I run a hand along his pale ghost body. He is both solid and made of cool winter air, and sometimes I swear I can feel his ears beneath my palm, while other times my fingers pass right through. He is both here and not here. Alive and dead. And right now he feels like my only friend—the only one who thinks I'm unchanged. Made of the same linen and blue thread.

Everyone else in Halloween Town seems to think I am someone entirely new—a girl with a royal title whose hair should be like the silken threads of a spider's web, with coffin-straight posture and a crown of feathers atop her head. But I am not these things.

The leafless branches of the forest cast long vertebrae shadows across the ground, and I tear away the black chiffon fabric pinned over my patchwork dress, leaving it in a heap behind me. I rip off the crown and toss it into a thornbush, where it snags on a branch, hanging there like tinsel on a tree. With Zero zipping along beside me, I break into a run, wanting to feel the cold night wind against my patchwork seams. Needing to feel the distance between myself and the town.

The sky is speckled with needle pricks of starlight, and even though the moon is hidden beyond a low layer of clouds, I know the path ahead through the trees. I follow it down a low gully, then up the other side, where the branches hang and stoop like old cobwebs after it rains. The air turns cool, and at last I arrive at the grove of seven trees—the place where Jack and I stepped through the heart-carved tree into Valentine's Town.

As if my legs have led me here without real purpose.

Zero hovers nervously beside me, looking back down the path the way we came. He doesn't like it here, in the dark of the trees, so far from town. But I walk into the center of the grove, running my palm down the trunk of each tree, feeling their carved bark made smooth by each symbol: a green four-leaf clover, an egg decorated in hues of pink and blue. I stop at the rose-red heart—the entrance into Valentine's Town. I could open the doorway and slip back into its realm. I could escape for a day or two, pretend I am someone else. Maybe I could even find Ruby Valentino, tell her that I'm not sure I want to be a queen—*that I don't even know how*—and she will offer up some advice to calm this ache in my chest. This nagging, prodding sense that perhaps I am living the wrong life.

Maybe I don't belong in either place. In either life. A girl in Dr. Finkelstein's lab or a queen.

I touch the shiny golden doorknob, already smelling the sugary sweetness—the hint of caramel and rose petals—when Zero lets out a quick high-pitched bark.

I drop my hand, turning.

But he's nowhere in sight.

The wind sails among the branches, and he barks again, somewhere beyond the grove of trees. Deeper into the woods. I follow the sound, across a barren stream, through dead autumn leaves where no path marks the way, into a part of the forest where I've never been.

A darker part.

A quieter part.

Where even the shadows have no shape. Where even the crows don't dare roost. Only darkness lives here, in the eerie calm and quiet of these bare trees.

Curiosity will be the devil of you, or the death, whichever comes first, Dr. Finkelstein told me once. It was a warning to keep my restless mind from wandering into places it didn't belong. To stay quiet and stay put.

But I was never any good at either.

Zero barks again, an excited yip–like he's found a freshly rotted bone–and I step around a thicket of thorny vines. But when I spot him, it's not a bone or a carcass he's standing over: he's facing a clot of brambles and briars. Nothing that seems like anything. Nothing out of place.

"Come on, Zero," I call, patting my leg.

But he begins tugging at the interwoven vines,

biting at the long-dead brambles and yanking them back.

I step closer, squinting through the dark, wishing I'd brought a candle.

And then, at last, through the strange formless shadows, I see it: a tree.

But not just any spiny tree. Something is carved into the trunk–a smooth, purposeful etching just like the seven trees in the grove.

I begin yanking away the last of the briars, thorns snagging at my linen flesh, my bare legs, pulling at my seams . . . but I keep going. I need to see. I need to know for sure.

And when enough of the choking vines have been torn away, I blink. *Refocus.* To be sure it's real.

A blue crescent moon has been carved into the rough, worn surface of the bark.

It's a tree like the others.

A doorway.

An entrance into another town.

The doorknob is knotted with vines—it hasn't been used for many years—and I have to tug away the dead coils, breaking them and tossing them aside. The sound of snapping wood echoes through the forest while Zero hovers beside me, ears raised, anxious to see what we've uncovered.

Once the edges of the door have been exposed, brambles and green scattered at my feet, I take in a deep breath and reach for the doorknob, pulling the door slowly open.

In an instant, the wind catches the oval-shaped door—a sudden gust, as if by magic or malediction—and flings it wide. I stagger back, grabbing one of the vines to keep my balance before pitching headlong into a thorny tiger's eye bush. Blinking, I sweep the hair back from my face and peer into the dark cavern of the open doorway.

Zero zips close, whimpering, sniffing this strange, unknown tree.

The doorway smells of lavender, of freshly brewed chamomile tea, and my doll eyes flutter, suddenly heavy, like silver coins placed on the eyelids of the dead.

I feel the soft, dreamy tug of a gentle wind.

Easy and quiet. Like bedding down in a knoll of moss, or sinking into a cellar, without sound. How easily I could tip forward and tumble headfirst through the doorway, into the hollowed-out tree. I blink. I run my fingertips along the edge of the doorway, feeling the roughness of the bark, the dark interior beckoning me. I swallow, starting to ease my way inside, one leg stepping through, head craned into the hollow, endless darkness . . . when Zero tugs against my arm.

I feel him pulling against me, the low growl from his throat, but my mind is lost to the quiet of the doorway. The hum of wind in my ears. *What is this place?* I wonder. *What waits on the other side?*

Zero bites harder, yanking against my fabric flesh, and I begin to hear the breaking of threads as the seam across my shoulder starts pulling apart.

"Zero," I say softly, my voice slipping, *slipping,* from my throat, lost to the dark cavern of the doorway. Noiseless and numb. Like an echo singing against my skin. But then I feel the sudden *pop, pop, pop* as the row of threads along my shoulder break apart, giving way, and my arm snaps free of my body.

I jolt backward, landing against the hard, cold ground with a thud.

For a moment, the sky is a kaleidoscope of stars, sparks in my eyes, the air gone from my chest. But when I blink, tilting my gaze, I see my loose arm hanging above me, still in Zero's mouth. He eyes me strangely, impishly, letting out a soft whimpering sound.

I gather the handful of dead leaves that have spilled from my open shoulder onto the ground: *the curse of being a rag doll; you can lose your insides easily.* But the cold of the forest tickles up my spine, a wind from somewhere deeper in the trees, and I feel a sudden dread—a prick of terror. I shouldn't be here, in this dark unknown part of the forest. An open, half-hidden doorway in front of me.

Zero barks, his voice muffled by my arm still clamped in his mouth.

I reach out for him, to retrieve my arm, but he flits just out of reach. "Zero, what are you doing?" I stand up awkwardly, then move toward him. But he drifts farther up the path, as if this is a game and now I'll have to catch him. "Zero!" I call, but he's moving faster now, zipping up the path, darting through the trees.

We reach the Hinterlands, but Zero keeps going, zigzagging through the bony elms to the edge of the forest. Dried leaves flutter out from my shoulder, leaving a trail behind me as I run. We cross the narrow bridge, through the gate into Halloween Town, and it's not until we reach the cemetery when Zero finally drops my arm onto the cold ground.

His tongue wags from his mouth, and he makes an excited little yip, but I shake my head at him. "Bad dog," I say softly, not truly meaning it, then slump down beneath Spiral Hill, where Jack and I were married only a day ago.

I pull out the blue spool of thread and the sharp needle I always keep in the left pocket of my dress—because old seams have a way of popping, thread unspooling, and you never know when you'll need it—and begin stitching my arm back into place. It takes longer than usual; some of the linen has begun to fray along the seam, and

I need to gather a few spare dead leaves from the graveyard to fill my shoulder socket all the way. It's a ghastly thing to lose an arm—or any part of yourself, really—to feel disconnected from your body. Not quite whole. And I've always wished Dr. Finkelstein had stuffed my insides with something other than dried, shriveled leaves, tossed aside by the trees. Cotton perhaps, or rose petals. Something silken and ladylike.

Once I've tied the string into a knot and broken the end with my teeth, I sink back against the curve of Spiral Hill, the moon full in the sky, the hour well after midnight, and I know I need to go find Jack. I will tell him about the other tree, the secret doorway beyond the Hinterland grove. And I will tell him something else—that I cannot be the queen the Mayor and the Witch Sisters and the Vampire Prince want me to be. I know what they expect of me: a proper wife, a proper Pumpkin Queen. But none of it feels like me. I will tell Jack about the gnawing ache between my fabric ribs, and he will see in my eyes that I need things to stay the same. He will kiss my cheek, my hand, and tell me that he'll set things right. He'll weave his fingers through mine and promise that nothing will have to change. *Ever.*

I let my eyes slip closed, feeling the cold night air against my overheated skin. I let myself imagine that Jack and I are back in the little cottage beside the chocolate river. Just the two of us. No Witch Sisters, no All Hallows' Eve party to plan, only the silence of his breath in my ear. Only the quiet, *quiet, quiet.*

And nothing else.

Nothing at all.

5

The sun has begun to rise, a blazing orange
pumpkin tottering against the hazy
skyline.

I wake with a jolt, scrambling to my feet. I've
been gone all night! Surely Jack's been worried,
pacing the house, wondering what's happened
to me.

Zero, who must have fallen asleep next to me,
makes cartwheel loops around me, anxious, and
we leave the cemetery, making our way past the
old, lopsided tree house where Lock, Shock, and

Barrel live. Their claw-foot bathtub sits in the leech grass below the tree house, but as I get closer, I see that it's not empty. There's something inside. Or, *somethings*.

Lock, Shock, and Barrel—all three of them—are slumped in the white porcelain tub. Eyes closed. And they're snoring loudly like the undead.

They're *asleep*.

In their bathtub.

I peer over the edge of the tub, curious. It's well after sunup, and Lock, Shock, and Barrel are usually stirring up mischief at the first sign of daylight. They don't want to miss a single hour of mayhem-making, ghost torturing, and pumpkin tipping. So why are they still asleep?

Their Halloween masks lie at their feet, and their real faces are strained—like they were caught mid-laugh, mid-scream, at the moment they fell asleep.

"Shock?" I say, nudging her in the shoulder.

But she only grumbles drowsily, then slumps deeper into the bathtub.

As I lean closer, I notice something else.

Sand.

They're covered in it: in their hair, down the sleeves of their shirts, even on their masks. This might seem strange, except nothing with Lock, Shock, and Barrel is ever that unusual. I wonder what sorts of tricks they've been up to. Out playing in a bog of sand somewhere, and now they're so tired they can't even blink an eyelid open.

Zero's nose twitches, but he doesn't move any closer to the tub. He prefers to steer clear of Boogie's Boys, as does nearly everyone in Halloween Town.

I leave the trio to their sleep, and continue on up the gray stone path. But the closer I get to the edge of town, I feel the leaves in my chest begin to clamber up into my throat, a knot of nerves, anxious, knowing that as soon as I'm spotted—seen by Corpse Kid or Mummy Boy or any of the others—a crowd will gather around me, tugging at my already-frayed arm, snapping out-of-focus photos. *Queen, queen*, they will shout. The Witch Sisters and the Vampire Prince will drag me back to my home, where they will resume their prodding and poking—likely furious with me for running away.

I quicken my pace up the path, hoping to make it home unseen.

But when I enter the eastern edge of town, and hurry down the alleyway behind the old, slanted toolshed where the Behemoth makes his home—sleeping on a too-small cot between graveyard shovels and pickaxes—I sense the quiet.

The chill of no voices, no footsteps.

I step through the long, silent shadows of the alley, and into the town square.

The air is perfectly still, silent as a morgue.

No wind howling through hollow doorways, no rattling bones from the skeleton tree, no accordion or saxophone echoing up the streets from the Corpse Band. The town should be bustling and hectic with Halloween less than two weeks away, cobwebs and ghost-silhouettes being constructed, screams to be practiced, gravestones carved, and coffins heaved up from the cemetery.

The town should be a jostling chorus of activity.

Instead, it feels like a place populated by the dead. The *real* dead. The never-going-to-rise-again kind of dead.

Zero hovers close at my side, sensing something isn't right.

Carefully, quietly, I walk to the center of the town square. *What did Lock, Shock, and Barrel do?* I think. They must be to blame for whatever has happened.

A troubling ache stirs in the pit of my stomach, where lost pins and threads gather in a tangle. Sometimes poking me from the inside out, warning me when something doesn't feel quite right.

But then, across the town square, I spot the Vampire Prince and his three vampire brothers, all slumped beside the jagged stone edge of the fountain, their four ruby-black umbrellas lying on the ground beside them, still open, but useless, while the morning sun shines against the vampires' pale, delicate faces.

I run to the Vampire Prince's side, my shoes clacking against the stones, and kneel down to touch his small white hand, fingernails grown out into sharp points—the better to puncture his victim's throats and drain them of their blood.

A soft sputter leaves his lips, chest rising with

an inhale. He's asleep, along with his brothers, just like Lock, Shock, and Barrel.

I frown, unsure why they'd be sleeping out here, beneath the cruel sun, when I notice something scattered over their inky black capes: a grittiness that dusts the ground, and their translucent skin.

I run my fingers along the edge of the Vampire Prince's cape, feeling the tiny grains that cling to the fabric.

Sand.

Just like I found in the bathtub with Lock, Shock, and Barrel.

The breath catches in my chest, and I stand up, taking a staggering step back. *This feels all wrong.* Even in a place like Halloween Town—where the darkness can make sinister shapes of the most humdrum objects, where a cool wind is always nibbling at the back of your neck—finding the Vampire Brothers and Lock, Shock, and Barrel all sound asleep feels like a different *type* of wrong.

A slipped-down-a-dark-*dark*-rabbit-hole kind of wrong.

"Why are they all asleep?" I say to Zero.

He floats over the brothers, sniffing at their closed eyelids, which remind me of black theater curtains pulled shut. Then Zero turns, quickly darting back to my side. The layer of sand, the sleeping vampires—it's all frightened him for some reason. And it's starting to frighten me.

I lift my gaze, blowing out a slow, silent breath, and up the street, I notice someone slumped against the steps of Town Hall.

There are more.

I'm starting to think that Lock, Shock, and Barrel didn't have anything to do with this, after all.

I cross the town square quickly, and find the Mayor half-sitting, one elbow bent against the hard stone steps. He looks like he could be sunbathing, soaking up the golden morning light, except his eyes are shuttered closed and there's a fine layer of sand scattered over him—just like the others. I touch his arm, carefully, and he teeters to one side, wobbles a bit like he's going to slide all the way down the stone steps, but then his body settles again.

Still, he doesn't wake.

My fingers hover over the sleeve of his coat, wanting to touch the grains of sand, scoop them up into my palm and feel their weight. I need to understand what it is. But something in me resists—screams at me to leave the sand where it is.

Something is terribly, awfully wrong.

I find Helgamine and Zeldaborn asleep in front of their Witch Sisters' Apothecary, Helgamine with her broomstick still clutched in her fingers. I don't bother trying to wake them; I'd rather let them sleep, anyway.

Wolfman is dozing softly beside the path that leads up to Dr. Finkelstein's observatory, his exhales muttering words I can't make out. I continue past him without thinking, my feet carrying me back to the place that was once my home, and I push open the door into Dr. Finkelstein's lab before I've even realized where I am. I find Dr. Finkelstein sitting at his worktable, a strange tilt to his head, a broken test tube on the floor—glass shattered around his chair. Igor, his assistant, is hunched in the corner, bone-biscuit crumbs on the floor all around him.

I step over Igor and head into the kitchen.

Dr. Finkelstein's wife, Jewel, is lying on her side next to the stove, a pot of something that smells like thyme and rotten eggs boiling over. I turn off the heat and try rousing Jewel with the toe of my shoe, but she makes only a faint snort, then resumes her impossibly deep sleep.

My chest tightens. *Wrong, wrong, wrong.* This is all wrong.

Dr. Finkelstein often accused me of too much daydreaming, a mind that swirled with fairy-tale thoughts. But I am also practical—logical. I like science and well-reasoned outcomes. But whatever has happened to the residents of Halloween Town doesn't make any sense. Potion or peril, some strange conjuring has put the whole town to sleep.

Yet for reasons unknown, *I* am still awake.

Zero hovers in the kitchen doorway, whimpering. He doesn't like the cold of Dr. Finkelstein's lab. He doesn't like any of this. He wants to see Jack.

Jack!

My leaves stir wildly in my chest, and I sprint from the lab and dart across the town square,

Zero flitting alongside me, past residents slumped and sagged and collapsed where they had stood.

I slam open the gate and run up the stone path to the house. The front door has been left ajar, and it thuds back against the wall as I push my way through. I check Jack's office first. Empty. His sketches and architectural plans for Halloween have been left scattered across the table; a few tumbled to the floor. I turn and run up the spiral stairs to our bedroom, my footsteps throwing echoes across the stone walls.

And when I find him, my stomach drops into my toes.

Jack is lying beside the open window that overlooks the town, black-moon eyes closed, mouth agape just slightly. *Dead asleep.*

I sink onto the floor next to him. "Jack?" I wipe away the fine layer of sand from his cold cheekbones, trying to hold down the sob in my chest. "Jack, please wake up!" I shake him, touching his face, trying to force his eyelids open. But he only makes a soft murmuring sound, mouth slack.

A desperate, panicked ache throbs against my eardrums, and I squeeze his limp hand. Finding the others asleep was unnerving, but seeing Jack lying beside the window, unmoving as the rest, makes me feel like I'm about to break open—dead leaves bursting through my fabric chest. Tears begin to stream down my cheeks, landing on the floor in tiny, salty puddles. "I need you to wake up!" I shake him again, desperately, but his arms hang like dead branches at his sides.

Zero drifts close to Jack, nudging him in the cheek. But it makes no difference.

Jack is asleep, just like the others.

And there is no waking him.

6

I wipe the tears from my face—the wetness
soaking into my linen skin—and drag Jack to
the bed, pulling him up onto our black patchwork quilt and placing his domed head carefully
on the pillow.

Zero hovers beside Jack, not wanting to leave
his side, whimpering softly, but I stand up and
walk to the French doors that open out onto the
terrace. The air is strangely quiet, the sun casting
late afternoon ribbons of light through the surrounding limbless trees, and I stand at the railing,

peering out over Halloween Town, trying to understand.

A coldness settles within me, a numbing ache, like passing through the cemetery and feeling a wayward ghost slip beneath the skin. Jack is asleep. The whole town is asleep. But why?

My mind circles back, retracing the moments that led me here.

When I fled Halloween Town, into the woods, everyone was still awake—bustling with preparations. But something happened while I was gone.

A riddle whispered in the dark, a riddle I don't have all the pieces to solve.

A mystery hidden in the grains of sand I found on Jack, and the others.

But in the silence, there is another thought, disloyal and traitorous, a stitch-deep feeling that creeps up from somewhere foreign inside my rib cage.

The quiet of Halloween Town is a relief.

There is an odd pleasure in the silence, in the lack of voices, in the cool air void of all sound.

I glance back through the doorway where

the yards of fabric from the Witch Sisters still lie across the floor, along with bat-wing hats and high-heeled shoes made of gargoyle bones and foul-smelling fish leather. I can still feel Helgamine's clawed fingers tugging through my not-quite-right hair, Zeldaborn pricking me with sewing pins, tucking and folding the fabric around my waist, across my chest. Poking new needle-holes along my flesh. I can still see the Mayor's frenzied glare as he rattled off my queenly duties; feel the eyes of the crowd as they shouted my name, tugging at my dress, the flash of a camera in my face. All of it like an autumn storm churning around me. As if I belonged to them now, a token queen to prod and touch.

But now . . . they are all asleep, and everything is perfectly, unexpectedly, wondrously quiet.

For the first time since Jack and I returned from our honeymoon, my heart settles in my chest, the tension in my jaw softens—all of my threaded seams loosening just a little, like a corset being unknotted at the spine.

I am alone.

And the solitude feels like a warm bath I want to sink down into, toes curled, bubbles gathering and popping against my tired flesh.

I walk back inside our bedroom and gather up the yards of fabric and too-tall shoes, and I stuff it all into the closet—barely able to close the door against the gathered hoard.

The breath in my chest is suddenly, oddly, calm. My eyes glance around the bedroom as if seeing it for the first time—a room that is just a room. Not a royal jail.

Soothed by the unnatural quiet, I move through the tomb-silent house, touching the black widow wallpaper and carved magpie chandeliers. In the kitchen, I brew a cup of black murkweed tea, the sound of the kettle the only noise echoing along the narrow walls. I stand on the front porch, gazing out at the noiseless town, watching the moon begin to rise, a full bone-white orb. Day turning to night.

It feels selfish somehow, a crime, these stolen moments of silence. Especially with Jack asleep upstairs—the one person I wish was standing beside me, savoring this unexpected quiet.

But just for a moment, I let myself imagine what it might be like to walk down the streets alone, without the eyes of others judging every tilt of my head, or the somber slant of my mouth, calling me by the name that is a knife against my eardrums: *Queen*. I could read every last book in Jack's library without a single interruption, gather herbs from the garden without anyone scolding me for the dirt on my royal shoes or the hem of a newly sewn gown. It feels indulgent to long for such things. To wish for a time before a sovereign title sat weighted on my shoulders like moorstones dredged up from the fountain.

But leaning against the porch railing, I let my doll eyes drift closed, listening to the soundless echo that stretches over Halloween Town. The stirring of leaves, the hiss of the cold autumn wind.

And nothing else.

By some peculiar working of magic, I have gotten exactly what I wanted.

Silence.

To be left alone.

But for how long?

My eyes flit open as I breathe in the evening air, when a sound reaches my ears. Soft and muted. I squint through the dark, and notice the stray black cat—a cat that often wanders the streets at night—appearing from the shadows, slinking around the bars of the iron gate in front of the house. She lets out a little mewing sound, and I hurry down the stone steps. When I kneel beside her, she arches her back, letting me run my fingers along her inky-black coat. "Were you here when everyone fell asleep?" I murmur to her.

She purrs from deep within her gut.

I scratch at her ears, wishing she could tell me what she saw, what happened here while Zero and I were in the woods. But then her pointed ears twitch away from me, watchful eyes cast out toward the town square. She hears something. *Or sees something.*

Then . . . I hear it, too.

A sound that begins as a low *shush, shush,* like water against gravel.

I stand up. Perhaps someone else is still awake. Cyclops, or Undersea Gal.

Cautiously, I push open the gate, and take a few small steps into the open.

The sound grows closer. *Shush . . . whoosh.* I open my mouth to call out, to ask who is there—who might still be awake—when the black cat suddenly darts away, through the metal gate, and vanishes into the dark alley behind the house.

My eyes rove across the town square, trying to see what's there.

But the murk of shadows and wind make tricks of the dark: a statue or wall comes into focus only to be swallowed up again by the night a moment later; a tree limb looks like a giant's hand, reaching long across the street. None of it real. None of it something to fear.

Until—

It comes into view . . . a *thing* appearing from the far corner of Town Hall.

At first, it's hard to describe, to separate from the night. It has the quality of moonlight—pale and shadowy all at once, as if it's made of a semidarkness, that moment just after twilight. It hovers just slightly above the ground—a foot or two, maybe a little more. A man-shaped creature—two arms and two legs—with a long white beard, long enough to fall well below his waist, and wisps of white hair sticking up wildly from his head. He's wrapped in a layered garment the color of clouds—soft whitish gray, similar to a cloak or a robe, folded around his tall, spindly frame in a way that's hard to tell where the fabric begins and ends.

He has the appearance of an old wise man who might be prone to telling tall tales late into the night, or one who might walk—or float—with a cane and drink large cups of Swamp Gray tea while he recounts the stories of his youth. But his face tells a different story.

He looks as if he's just crawled up out of an open coffin, thick, unkempt eyebrows sloped together, mouth punctuated downward, with creases cut into his forehead, and dark, crescent-moon shadows sagging beneath both eyes.

He reminds me of the undead—newly risen.

And from where I stand in the shadows, I think perhaps that's what he is. One of the old bodies buried in the cemetery, risen a few days too early, before All Hallows' Eve. An accidental awakening. Maybe his eyes snapped open while he was still clamped shut inside his coffin, and he was forced to dig his way free to the surface. Surely anyone would look as terrifying after finding themselves buried six feet under the ground, with no ladder or shovel in sight.

I soften my gaze–feeling suddenly sorry for the poor fellow–and watch as he rounds Town Hall, drifting closer to the fountain.

I'm about to step out from the shadow where I'm hidden, when I notice something spilling out behind him: soft flecks that catch in the dull moonlight. Like tiny falling stars.

Like . . . sand.

The air falters in my throat, and I sink back into the dark. Into the shadow beside the gate.

Sand.

The floating, white-haired man reaches the Witch Sisters, then leans over them, as if testing to see if they're really asleep. He pokes a finger at Helgamine's nose, then peers at Zeldaborn's bird-like eyes, watching for any movement. He reaches into a hidden pocket inside his pale robe, then puffs up his cheeks, blowing a long breath across his palm. A cloud of shimmery white sand engulfs Zeldaborn's face, raining down around her.

The white-haired man waits a moment, watching. But Zeldaborn doesn't stir, doesn't twitch, doesn't wake: she is fully, inextricably asleep. Satisfied, the man-creature spins around and promptly leaves the town square, drifting in the direction of Dr. Finkelstein's observatory.

I try not to move—to make even the tiniest of sounds—as I watch him disappear into the dark.

I suck in a breath, then another, eyes unable to blink—wanting to be sure he's really gone; then I turn and bolt up the steps, back into the house. All my threads clench along my seams, my stomach twisted and sharp, and I race up the spiral stairs, nearly stumbling on the top step, then scramble into our bedroom. Zero is still hovering over Jack's sleeping body, refusing to move. I sink down onto the bed. "Jack!" I hiss, kneeling over him, arms shaking. My eyes flick to the window, watching for the gray-haired man. "Jack! There's something out there." I grab his shoulders with both hands, rattling him, urging him to wake. *Pleading*. But he only flops in my arms, then slumps back onto the bed. His white skull unmoving.

Tears break over my eyelids, and a white-hot panic rises into my chest—a feeling that begins to flood through my entire body. *Fear.* And something else: a rotting, terrible, knife-edged guilt.

I had thought it wasn't so bad, letting everyone sleep. Just for a little while. It had felt like a gift, like the midnight stars had bestowed this unusual quiet on me.

But now I understand.

It was never Lock, Shock, and Barrel who did this, as I'd first thought.

Everyone is asleep . . . because there is a monster in Halloween Town.

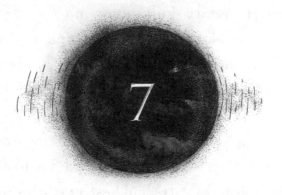

7

The garden is sunk into a shadowless dark. A full, unending kind of dark that seeps into every corner of the fence line, every leaf and stem and bleeding thorn.

I waited until I saw the gray-bearded man drift out toward the cemetery at the farthest edge of town, before slipping from the house and running along the stone wall to the garden behind Dr. Finkelstein's observatory, keeping out of sight.

Now my leaves churn in my chest as I gather the herbs. Knowing I will need to be quick.

I fill a metal pail with ginseng, sage, and bacopa. I pull up a clump of morning root and coffee basil, and when my pail is full, I slink along the outer wall of the garden. In the distance, I can still hear the creature, though I can't see him. The town is so quiet, so motionless, that even his faint muttering sounds echo back to me. He is humming a tune, a *lullaby*, I think. Soft and alluring. And I wonder if he senses that there is someone still awake in Halloween Town—someone he hasn't yet found—and is trying to coax me into the open.

I hurry back up the stone path to the house—before his cajoling words can drift into my ears, into my thoughts, making me forget what I need to do—and close the door quietly behind me.

In the dimly lit kitchen at the back of our house, where a single stove and a tiny, lopsided icebox sit pressed against one wall, I begin to brew the herbs in a pot of mud-water. I listen for any sound of the bearded figure beyond the walls while I stir the boiling mixture, the kitchen filling with its potent, heady scent. When the herbs have been steeped of all their color, and the brew looks like chalky-gray milk, I pour it into a porcelain mug and carry it up to our bedroom.

Jack is just as I left him—motionless on the bed—and I lift his head in my palm, careful to slowly pour the warm brew into his mouth and down his throat, not wanting to spill a drop. When the mug is empty, I place my palms against his chest, waiting for him to stir awake, for his black bottomless eyes to flutter open and peer up at me.

"Please," I whisper, so softly I know he won't be able to hear. Tears stream over my threaded eyelids, falling onto his cheeks. "Jack." My voice breaks, desperate, pleading. I need him to squeeze my hand, to wake up and wipe the tears from my face. I thought I wanted to be alone, but now I see the flaw in it—the gaping, awful wound. To be alone means to *feel* alone. To stand in a place that should be bustling with noise, and hear only the soft exhale of your own shallow breath.

I was wrong.

And I need Jack to wake up.

The old grandfather clock in the hall ticks

each second loudly in my ears. *It's taking too long.* The leaves in my chest fall silent, the lost needles in my stomach stab at my flesh.

The potion I made should have been strong enough to wake the crankiest of the dead from the oldest coffins. Jack should have sat up straight, eyes shot wide, when the first drop trickled down his throat.

But after another minute passes, and the brewed herbs simply turn his pale cheekbones a dull, watery pink, I know it's not going to work. All the hope I had felt inside me feels like it has spilled out onto the floor, now a puddle of pain.

He's not going to wake.

I release my hand from his chest and sink back onto my heels, looking to the window—the cool night breeze mussing the curtains—while dread slithers up and down my patchwork seams.

If my potion won't wake Jack, if I can't undo whatever the creature has done to him and the others, then I am truly, terrifyingly all alone.

Outside the house, the humming begins to grow louder.

A drowsy tune, childlike, like a melody sung to babies before sleep. But this song is not like the ones we sing in Halloween Town—about howling ghosts and creepy *creep*s who lurk under beds and claw out your eyes while you sleep. The song this monster sings is one of soft summer clouds and white-cotton sheep who graze in cornflower meadows and rest under pink starry skies.

I slink to the bedroom window, my small shoes hardly making a sound on the floorboards, and peer outside. The lullaby echoes over the black stone rooftops, drawing closer like a phantom beneath the pale moonlight. The lump in my throat tightens, and I start to turn back to Jack . . . when something slips past the window outside. A soot-dark shadow. Awful and fleeting and much too close.

Stumbling over my own feet, I scramble behind the curtain, hands pressed to the wall behind me.

But I wasn't fast enough.

I can see the silhouette of the bearded figure through the curtain, hovering just outside the window. Sand spills from his robe pockets, making a soft *tink, tink, tink* sound on the stone path below. And for the first time, his humming melody reshapes into words, whispered through the dark. *"The night is warm and drowsy, and you must be tired,"* he croons. *"Step into the open, and I will give you what you desire."*

I sink down to the floor and cover my ears with my palms. I don't want to hear his words; I don't want to slip into a deathly sleep like Jack and the others. Zero is cowering behind the closet door and I want to run to him, but I'm afraid of being seen.

"I am not the thing you fear," he whispers now. *"I am the giver of dreams. Of riddles and lullabies and moonbeams."*

I swallow down the terror climbing up my throat like a storm of leaves, whipping around inside my chest. I can't stay here, by the open window. But before I can stand up and run for the doorway, a great gust of wind tears into the bedroom, and with it comes a cloud of white flecks, like spun sugar.

Sand.

It rains across the bedroom floor, it falls against my hair, it settles into the cracks in the floorboards, and in my throat. I cough, despite myself, and the creature quickly ceases its humming.

Now he knows for sure: there's someone inside the room.

He's found me.

I have to run. *Now.*

I push myself up, shoes slipping on the fine layer of sand. I almost fall, but scramble to the closet and yank open the door. Inside, Zero is shaking, terrified.

"We have to go!" I hiss at him.

His pumpkin nose has dimmed, but he slips free of the closet, and we duck out into the hall, racing down the stairs toward the front door. I grip the doorknob and yank it open, about to dart out into the twilight, but the creature's shadow slips by overhead.

He's circling the house, looking for us.

The leaves in my chest claw up into my throat, beating behind my teeth, making everything vibrate with fear. I try to slam the door closed, but there is another gust of wind, and the door swings wide, crashing against the wall with a loud *crack*, throwing me and Zero back into the hallway.

In an instant, the creature is in the doorway–staring down at me.

We peer at one another, eye to eye.

"Sleep, sweet child, your dreams are close, your pillow as soft as a downy rose." His words are slow and plying, as gentle as fingertips across silk.

I pause, legs frozen beneath me, as the creature slips across the threshold only a few feet away, humming under his breath. His eyes are settled on mine, but they seem subdued: doughy and soft, less sinister somehow. Just an old gray-haired man, singing songs to calm rattled minds.

I could rest a while, I think. Sink onto the floor of the hallway and listen to the ease and lull of each of his languid words. Let my bustling mind slow, and sleep for only a moment or two.

But Zero nudges my palm and growls. I blink, snapping my gaze away.

The creature is inside the house, and I've stalled in the hallway like a doll who's lost all her stuffing.

I swallow, shaking away the feeling of his

words in my ears—the buttery calm humming through every stitch and seam—and I turn, Zero at my heels, then sprint down the hall, our only option. At the far end of the hallway, I slip into Jack's library.

A single window—narrow and rarely opened—sits in the back corner, framed by bookshelves.

I don't have a choice.

Zero watches anxiously as I shimmy the window up in its frame, then squeeze myself through the opening. I can hear the creature moving down the hall, hissing his lurid lullaby—trying to beckon me forth. Yet he doesn't move quickly, in no great hurry; he knows that sooner or later his victims can no longer resist his words, and they sink into a listless, muddled haze.

He reaches the doorway to Jack's library, and makes a dissatisfied sound—like teeth mashing together, impatient and irritated—when he sees me half perched in the window.

The drop is far—several stories from atop Skull Hill, where our house is perched high above the ground—but I snuck out of countless windows when I lived in Dr. Finkelstein's lab. So I suck in a breath, then launch myself out the open window, sailing through the night air until I hit the ground far below with an abrupt *smack*.

The fall would kill most people—crack apart delicate, porous bones. Luckily, I have no bones to break.

Zero flutters through the open window, his ghost-body drifting down to me, then noses me in the cheek.

"I'm okay," I whisper.

My left leg has twisted backward at the knee, but there's no time to mend it, so I scramble upright, balancing on one good leg. Above me, the creature hasn't reached the window quite yet, but we need to run before he sees us—before he knows which way we've gone.

Limping, I stagger away from the house into the shadows of the alleyway, Zero beside me, and I can still hear the creature banging through the halls, pushing open doors, searching. I circle around the back of the house, leg hitching awkwardly, and hurry up the path through the cemetery, across the bridge, and into the woods. Into the dusky cover of darkness.

But we're only a few paces into the trees, when Zero nips at my elbow, tugging at my fabric.

Out of breath, I stop and spin around to look at him, his ghost-dog fur a stark white against the dark of the forest, and he whimpers at me.

"What's wrong?" I whisper.

He releases my elbow and turns his watery gaze back the way we came, toward town, and our house in the distance. His dog ears sag, nose dimmed . . . and then I understand.

He doesn't want to leave Jack.

"We can't go back there," I tell him. "That . . . *thing* will put us both to sleep, and then there will be no one left awake." I think about the sand that blew in through the window, how it's already settled in my hair, my throat. It might only be a matter of time until I slip into an unwaking slumber. Unless I brushed it from my skin in time, shed it clean. Or perhaps it was only a small dusting, not nearly enough to put me to sleep. Either way, I'm not going to stay and find out. I'm not going to risk it happening again.

Zero makes another sad, desperate sound, eyes

cast up the path, through the cemetery, to where Jack lies asleep on the second floor of our home. I run my hand along Zero's neck, stroking his ghostly fur. "I understand," I say quietly. *He wants to stay with Jack. He won't leave him behind, alone.* No matter what. He nudges his head into my cheek, and I lower my hand. "I'll come back," I assure him, although I don't know how; I just know I need to get away from Halloween Town before that creature finds me again. I need to get somewhere safe.

Zero lifts his ears, makes a small whining sound, then flits away, back toward the edge of the trees. But before he passes over the bridge, he pauses to look back at me, and I nod, holding down the anxious lump in my throat, the urge to call out to him—not wanting to leave him behind—but he disappears through the shadowed cemetery, out of sight.

He is loyal to Jack, even now. And although there is an edge of fear inside me, leaving him like this, I also know he'll be able to stay hidden from the creature, quiet and ghostly. He'll keep to the shadows at the back of the closet. And some part of me is grateful that he's staying behind—with Jack.

I wish I could, too.

But I can hear the creature's lullaby echoing through the streets of town, sailing on the wind, still searching for me.

I need to get far away from here.

I turn away from Zero and Jack and all of Halloween Town, and I hobble deeper into the shadowy woods, as fast as my twisted leg will carry me, until the town is lost behind me. Until there's only the dark eerie quiet of the trees, and the fluttering of my dead leaves.

8

The woods are oddly still.

No wind. No Mourning Owls crying from the treetops.

The moon cuts longways through the spiny forest, and I follow the path until I reach the familiar grove of trees—not knowing where else to go, where to hide. I sink down onto the dry ground in a stretch of shadows. My knee has suffered two torn stitches from the fall, and I brace my leg with both hands, then yank it back around so my foot is facing forward, before I quickly stitch the seam back together—while my eyes dart up the path, watching for the creature. Listening for his unnaturally soothing song echoing through the forest.

Using my teeth, I snap the end of the thread, then scramble to my feet, testing out the leg. It was a hasty mending, but it'll have to do.

I survey the grove of trees—everything just as it was the night before.

But I move past it, deeper into the woods, remembering the way to the wall of briars that concealed the newly discovered tree. *The unknown tree.* Perhaps it will be a safe place to hide, away from the worn path that cuts through the forest. But when I reach the lone tree, the air escapes my throat.

The moon-carved doorway into the tree . . . is wide open.

The dark hole like a child's yawning mouth.

I never closed the door. I left it open.

The cold realization slams into my stomach. When I found the door, I'd been distracted, trying to retrieve my torn arm from Zero's mouth as he fled the woods, racing after him back to the cemetery.

My mind tumbles against another thought, not wanting it to be true. Maybe it's a coincidence: the open door and the bearded man-creature who has put everyone in Halloween Town to sleep. I want to believe these two things aren't connected, that it isn't my fault.

But the twisting in my knotted stomach, in the base of my throat, tells me that it is.

I have let something *out* into our town.

I did this.

I step forward quickly and slam the little door—afraid of what else might be waiting on the other side. I gather dead branches and broken limbs from the forest floor, securing them across the doorway, making a hasty barricade.

A way to keep out any other monsters that might slither or creep or crawl through.

The woods feel too quiet, the darkness heavy. Guilt crashes through me like a guillotine cutting down to bone. There is no one else to blame, no one to unleash my anger upon for being so foolish and stupid. I have left the door open into some unknown world and unleashed a creature into Halloween Town.

I pick at the thread on my wrist as another thought begins to fester in my mind: The aloneness rotting in my chest taking on a new meaning. Clear and undeniable.

There is no one else to undo what's been done. No one left but me.

With Halloween less than two weeks away, it's not only the residents of Halloween Town who I have doomed, but all of Halloween. If I don't find a way to wake the others, there will be no pumpkins burning bright on doorsteps, no ghosts rattling chains from children's bedroom closets, no tricks unleashed on All Hallows' Eve night. Not this year. Not ever.

This is my fault.

With my head pulsing, my knee still a little off-center, I walk the several yards back to the original grove of seven trees. I stand in the middle, turning in a circle.

I know I can't stay here.

I can't risk the creature finding me, putting me to sleep. I narrowly escaped him once before. I might not be so lucky again.

And maybe...*maybe.* There will be someone in the other holidays who will know how to stop the bearded man with sand sifting from his pockets. I think back to Valentine's Town, our honeymoon—only days ago—and I wonder if Ruby Valentino will know how to send him back to where he came from. Surely she will have some queenly trick, or simple remedy to set things right.

I open the red heart doorway that leads to Valentine's Town, my fingers trembling.

I remember the hesitation I felt only days ago: I didn't want to leave Halloween Town, I was afraid to venture into a world I didn't know, but when Jack folded his cold fingers through mine, I knew I'd go anywhere with him.

Now I have to do this on my own.

I suck in a long, shaky breath, fear and courage stewing together inside me—making me feel light-headed—but I force myself to extend my crooked leg through the doorway, and then my arms, before tumbling headfirst into Valentine's Town.

There is nothing graceful about the descent into a new realm.

It's pinwheeling ribbons of starlight and little paper-white hearts. But when I land in Valentine's Town, I don't take the time to admire the heart-shaped trees and spun-sugar sky; I start immediately toward the town's borders.

But I sense the strangeness in the air as soon as I step through the iron-forged gate and hurry down the cobblestone streets. The center of town, at the cupid's fountain, is unnaturally quiet. The scent of melted chocolate and candy wax dripping from fingertips is all gone.

. The air smells flat, sugarless.

Like watered-down cake batter, left to spoil on the kitchen counter.

I start toward the Lovebird Inn, but I don't even make it a block before I see the first plump, rosy-cheeked woman asleep in a doorway, head canted to one side, a dozen tiny heart-shaped candies strewn on the ground by her hand. The words *My Honey B* and *Little Love* are stamped into the chalky hearts.

"Ma'am?" I say to the woman, but I already know, I sense . . . she won't wake. Just like the residents of Halloween Town, she too has been cast into an odd, otherworldly kind of slumber. Farther up the street, I find others, passed out at café tables, hot chocolate left cold beside their limp fingers, heads slumped against shoulders, eyes sunk closed, babies dozing in their strollers while their parents lie on the cobblestone sidewalk, also fast asleep. I find a cluster of cupids resting near the lazy chocolate river, little muttering sounds slipping from their cherry lips. They look like tiny confections, babies who've eaten too many sweets, wings gone still against their backs.

And every last one of them is covered in a soft dusting of white sand.

It's scattered across the streets, stuck in window frames and doorways and beneath fingernails.

It's everywhere.

I pass by delicatessens where candied gingers, marzipan almonds, and lemon macarons have been left in windowsills to rot in the morning sunlight. At last, I discover Ruby Valentino, asleep in the front garden of what must be her home, hedged roses and petunias blooming all around her. It's a well-tended garden—not a single bleeding heart flower in sight—and behind it stands a frosted pink house, tall and narrow like a high-heeled shoe. She still looks just as glossy and queenly as she did awake, but now her lips sputter with each exhale, and I bend down to touch her hand softly where she's lying in the flattened grass, a half-eaten chocolate truffle with butterscotch swirls a few inches from her lifeless fingertips.

"Ruby?" I whisper, hoping against all reason that she might wink a sleepy eye up at me and magically stir awake. I place my other hand on her shoulder and rock her gently, saying her name louder, several more times—my tone growing more frantic, more afraid. My voice echoes across Valentine's Town, up the empty streets, with no other sounds to break it apart. And the echo sends a spike of cold down to my tailbone.

Ruby's mouth hangs open, and I lower her back down to the grass, letting her sleep.

Valentine's Town is lost to a deep slumber.

And I'm starting to wonder if I'm the last one still awake . . . anywhere.

9

I hurry through the gates of Valentine's Town—hating the silence, the stilled air—and back into the shiny, rose-tinted forest. I think of Jack asleep in our bed, Zero waiting at his side, and I know I need to travel to the other holidays. I need to be sure. There must be someone awake in one of the towns, someone who can help me.

At the grove of trees, I touch the only other familiar door. A green tree etched into the wood with colorful bauble ornaments painted on the limbs, a star at the top, and ruby-red presents with gold ribbon set at the base of the tree. This door will take me to Christmas Town, the place Jack has visited several times. Maybe Sandy Claws will be able to help me—the cheerful, elven-like man who I once saved from Oogie Boogie.

I pull open the doorway and let the cold, snow-dusted wind pull me inside.

Jack has talked of Christmas Town many times: the layer of soft snow, the gingerbread house where Sandy Claws lives, the bustling townsfolk preparing for their holiday. But when I make my way into the town, lit by strings of tiny colorful lights, several small cottages lining the snowy streets, I find it unusually quiet—especially with Christmas a little more than two months away.

I listen for the singsong of voices, for the elves Jack described to me one night before we were married, when we sat beside the fireplace in his room, drinking slug-nettle tea as he told me stories of the other towns. His eyes seemed lit from within, even brighter than the firelight, as his hands waved in the air to describe every detail. He loved the other holiday towns, couldn't wait to share each one with me. But now . . . I'm starting to worry he won't get the chance. Now I'm traveling to the other holidays on my own, without him.

"Sandy Claws!" I call out, peering up each empty, snowy street. At last, I come to a rather large gingerbread house at the far end of town. I knock on the rounded door—decorated with white frosting and green tinsel—but there's no answer. Cautiously, I push open the door and step inside.

Across the living room, seated in an overstuffed chair beside a fireplace—the fire still crackling, hazelnuts roasting in a pot over the flames, and a cup of cocoa with tiny, bobbing marshmallows on the table beside him—is Sandy Claws. Asleep.

He looks rather peaceful, in fact, snoring quietly, mumbling to himself, a sprig of mistletoe hanging above him. I could easily be fooled into thinking he's simply taking a quick afternoon nap, except when I touch his hand and say his name, he doesn't startle awake. Instead, a cloud of sand spills from this thick red coat, onto the floor.

I back away from him, wiping my fingertips

across my dress—the same chill I felt in Valentine's Town clambering down my skin—and I slip back out through the doorway, into the snowy cold.

I enter a large gingerbread workshop a few yards away; three dozen tiny elves with bells in their hair and ribbons around their wrists—just like Jack described—are also asleep. The assembly of presents at a standstill, spun ribbons lying in heaps on the floor at their feet, no songs whistling from their lips while they work.

I close the door to the workshop and rush back toward the forest.

I turn in a circle, at the center of the grove of trees in Christmas Town, deciding.

My eyes settle on the giant egg, painted in pastel hues of peach and spring-sky blue. I remember the Easter Bunny, whom Lock, Shock, and Barrel accidentally kidnapped last winter. He seemed harmless enough, a creature who hopefully comes from a realm with nothing to fear, so I step forward and touch the shiny doorknob, my pulse quickening in my throat, and I pull open the door, stepping into the dark of the tree.

Pinwheeling through the doorway, I land in the warm, springlike forest of Easter Town. But beneath my palms, the grass feels all wrong. Woven and papery—not like grass at all. It even has a strange, pastel hue—as if it's been dyed using green clovers or swamp water—and it crunches beneath my black shoes as I walk up the meadow path toward Easter Town.

The air is muted and quiet, and my eyes scan the meadow for signs of anyone awake, but instead I find something else nestled among the tall grass and tucked along the squat wooden fence that borders the path: countless small eggs, all painted in shades of pastel—just like the doorway. They sit perched in the knobs of several oak trees, and along a border of blooming tulips, as if they've been hidden, and now are waiting to be found—plucked from the ground and kept as souvenirs or prizes. But I can't imagine why anyone would gather eggs of such unusual colors. Surely they're poisonous. If these eggs were discovered in

Halloween Town, there would certainly be some kind of malice or cruel trick waiting inside.

A thought—shutter-quick—enters my mind: *I wish Jack were here. He would know what the eggs mean. He would know if I should be afraid of this place.*

But I stuff down the unease and continue on up the path, where the gate into Easter Town arches up toward the perfectly pale sky, looking like a braided basket with a tall looping handle interwoven with daisies and poppies and other spring flowers.

This is an odd town, I think, as I pass through the gate. But I quickly realize... it's hardly a town at all.

There are no shops or buildings or a town square with a bubbling candy fountain. Only a massive wildflower meadow with holes dug into the earth—like warrens. Places where rabbits make their homes.

The path ends at a small gazebo—a squat wooden structure painted with yellow daisies and colorful tulips—mirroring the field of flowers that surrounds it. I edge closer to the gazebo, peering inside, where low wooden tables are lined with baskets—each filled with a dozen or so eggs, and the same odd grass from the forest. Glass jars with inky water sit alongside a dozen circular palettes of watercolors. This must be the place where the eggs I saw along the path are painted.

But there is something else inside the gazebo.

A dozen rabbits are gathered together, as if they clotted in the center of the open-air structure, terrified, before being overcome by a cloud of sand that knocked them unconscious.

And lying on the white-wood steps that lead up into the gazebo—as if he tried to fend off something as it drew closer—is a single rabbit larger than the others. His fur is buttery pink—like melted strawberry ice cream—and he wears a cream-white sash that reads *Happy Easter.*

He is asleep, just like all the others.

My fabric chest feels tight as I sprint back up the path to the woods, a new kind of panic burning in my throat, behind my eyes.

What if no one is awake?

Anywhere?

At the grove of trees, I choose another door–a large feathered turkey painted onto the bark– and before I can let the doubt and fear take root, I yank open the door and step through.

The wind is cold and bitter in this town, the scent of autumn in the air–leaves turning copper and shades of sunset. They crunch under my feet as I walk, and it almost feels like home–like Halloween Town–except with a hint of snow in the air. Winter creeping closer. A later season.

I follow the dirt path out of the woods, toward a crude wooden sign hanging over the town gate, creaking in the wind.

THANKSGIVING TOWN, it reads.

Already, the air feels too still, but I pass through the gate and down into a small valley where the town sits cradled by farmland and low hills on all sides. Crops of corn and wheat and even pumpkins line the surrounding fields. My shoes kick up dust as I walk down the main street, bordered by homes made of freshly cut logs, the scent of smoke hanging in the air, coiling up from chimneys. And for a moment, I think this is a sign that someone in this town might still be awake.

But there are no voices. No stirring footsteps. No one tending to the far fields.

It's just as abnormally quiet as every other town I've visited.

But at last, I do see someone.

A man is lying faceup on the front porch of a small log house. A carved pipe rests between his fingertips, the embers extinguished, and with each exhale, a soft sputter leaves his lips, making his mustache quiver. Through the open doorway behind him, I see others inside his home, seated along a long wooden table—as though they just sat down to dinner, except they are slumped forward in their wood chairs, foreheads pressed to plates— with bowls of soup steaming, coffee cups tipped over, forks still clutched in hands.

Sand at their feet.

After I found the secret, hidden door, after I ran to the cemetery and fell asleep beneath the pale full moon beside Spiral Hill, was the bearded man slipping through every doorway, into every town, putting every resident to sleep?

While I wandered through our house, feeling relief to finally be alone, savoring every quiet moment, was the creature sneaking through doorways?

I did nothing, while he tore through these helpless towns, blowing sand into the faces of everyone he found.

A chill slinks down each of my seams.

I did this.

The eerie hush of this town is bone-breaking—the quiet has crept into every corner and floorboard, nothing awake, nothing left—and I feel hollow as I hurry back into the woods, the nerve-frayed edges of my thoughts moving too quickly, cycling over and over the same idea: *What if I can't find a way to wake them? What if I'm the last one?*

I pass a flock of wild turkeys, darting through the trees, startled by my footsteps—making odd warbling sounds before they scurry away, quick and frightened. Quick enough that they managed to avoid the creature's sand.

When I reach the grove, I'm out of breath, the leaves in my chest stirring wildly, manically, like they might burst through my seams.

But I have to see this through.

I need to know for sure that there's no one else awake.

In Fourth of July Town, bright exploding lights shake the dark, starless sky.

But even for all the whirring, crackling noise, everyone I find is dozing quietly in their dome-shaped homes—ceilings all made of glass to see the perpetual night sky—and not even the pinwheels of colorful starlight erupting over the town can wake them.

It's just the same as all the other towns. Sand scattered across sleeping bodies, caught in their hair, some with eyes still open, as if watching the exploding sky above.

My own body shivers, vibrates, the dread becoming something else—a horrible knowing.

CHAPTER NINE

I might be the only one left. I sprint back to the woods, legs wobbling with each stride, because when I reach the grove, I know, there's only one town remaining.

10

At the grove, I step through the last remaining door—a green four-leaf clover etched and painted into the tree, the color of graveyard ferns.

My last hope.

When I step through the doorway, I find myself in a small forest, trees stunted and short, where the air smells of moss and mint. Surveying the surrounding trees, I notice several paths leading away from the grove, heading in different directions. Unlike the other holiday realms, where a single path led to the town, here there are many. Without pathway signs or markers, I have no way to know which path is the right one. But with no time to waste, I choose a path at random and start off into the woods.

The path takes me along a cool, rocky stream, then up a hillock, and down again, until at last, unexplainably, I find myself back in the grove of seven trees. Right where I started. I blow out a breath, forehead tensed, irritated, then I start down another path—because I don't have a choice. I follow it through a dense patch of hissing cattail reeds, over a rocky wall that might have once been a fence line, and then, impossibly, it leads me right back to the grove. Back to the beginning. As if I am caught in an endless, maddening loop.

Quickly, I survey the other paths, the ones I haven't yet taken, but I'm beginning to wonder if this is some kind of trick, a way to detour uninvited guests. To keep them from finding the town.

The sun is still high in the sky, a wall of rain clouds in the distance, but I decide to abandon the paths altogether, instead choosing to follow the long, fingerlike shadows cast down by the trees.

In Halloween Town, it's said that if you're ever lost, you should follow your own shadow... it will always take you where you need to go.

I push my hands into the pockets of my dress, lift my chin—feeling the seam along my neck tense—and step away from the grove, making my own trail through the thick underbrush and thorny leaves. I follow my lean shadow across the ground, down a long sloping hillside, across a grassy valley that smells of mint and hops, until, through the glittery sunlight, I see it.

A town.

Tucked into the shallow end of the long valley, surrounded by green fields.

I race through the tall grass licking at my exposed legs, until I reach a gold-hued gate, and I tilt my head up to read the sign: ST. PATRICK TOWN.

I found it.

I glance down at my shadow, nodding, then I hurry up the narrow main street, where tiny thatched-roof homes made of loam and gathered twigs crowd each side, pressed in close. Strangely, the doorways are half my size—too small for me to step inside. Instead, I crouch down and peer through glazed windows to see small kitchens with miniature teakettles squealing, beds unmade, biscuits burning in ovens left on.

The small glimmer of hope I felt when I found the town quickly darkens when I find small red-bearded men and rosy-cheeked women asleep inside tiny cafés and pubs. Pints undrank, green tea unsipped. I even find curly-haired babies resting in woolly, moss-made cribs.

"I'm too late," I say softly to myself as I reach the end of a row of tiny woodland structures, and I press my palms to my eyes to keep the tears from falling. There's no one left awake, no one who can help me. I drop my hands and squint up at the pale, glistening sky. Maybe I should return to Halloween Town, walk into the town square, and wait for the creature to find me. And when he does, arm outstretched with a fistful of sand, I won't flinch, I won't run away. I will close my eyes and feel the cloud of sand rain down over me, letting everything go dark. *Nothing but the dark.*

I will sleep like the others. Like Jack. And I won't be alone anymore.

Jack. At the thought of him, my unshed tears at last break over my eyelids, wet and cold, but I don't wipe them away. I let the weight of it all sink over me, the awful, cruel pain. The knowing guilt. *I did this.* I opened a doorway and allowed a monster into my world. *Your curiosity will kill you,* Dr. Finkelstein once told me. Maybe he was right. But instead of killing me, it's taken the man, the skeleton, I love.

The little town blurs from view, smeared by wetness, and I blink, *blink* . . . just as something darts in front of me.

A flash of green.

Of brown velvet shoes skittering away into a narrow dirt alleyway between buildings.

Someone is awake.

I brush my palm over my eyes, catching a last glimpse of the figure darting into the shadows. But it takes half a second for my legs to understand what my eyes are seeing, for my body to swing itself forward, to go after the small, half-sized man.

He dashes beyond the borders of town, through a wall of bracken ferns, and into a small glen where the grass grows tall and a winding stream churns over smooth river stones.

I'm out of breath when I finally catch up to him, the tears dried against my cheekbones. But the tiny man doesn't seem to notice me. He climbs atop a boulder, looking out over the blades of grass.

"Hello?" I say softly, my voice a rasp, my eyes struggling to believe that he's real—and awake.

"Have you seen it?" he calls back, not even looking at me, unfussed by my sudden out-of-nowhere appearance. He holds a hand above his eyes, scanning the glen.

I step closer to him, through the wavy ferns and tall grass. "Seen what?"

"The rainbow," he answers brusquely, his tone thick with annoyance. "It was just here . . . now it's gone."

I glance out over the glen. The air has a hint of rain to it, of dampness, and everything smells rich like soil. But I see no sign of a rainbow. "Why are you looking for a rainbow?"

The little man turns his gaze to me for the first time, and I see that his eyes are a golden color, his coiled beard gleaming copper red in the sunlight. "I'm not looking for the *rainbow*," he huffs, impatient. "I'm looking for the pot at the end of it."

I feel the seams at the corners of my mouth pull together, confused. His whole town is asleep, and yet he's worried about the location of some rainbow.

He shakes his head and hops down from the boulder, light and quick, feet landing in the soft soil. "I hid the pot somewhere in this glen, and now I can't find it." He scratches at his tightly coiled beard, turning one side of his mouth upward as if searching the lost places of his mind. "The rainbow will show me where I left it."

"What's in the pot?"

His eyes cast up to me, shivering in the damp sunlight. "My gold, of course." He says it like I should already know this—as if it were obvious. It reminds me of Ruby Valentino, how she assumed I would know about cupids and the burdens of being queen. But so far, I've found these other towns entirely foreign and strange, with people and customs that make no sense to me.

"I haven't seen a rainbow," I answer, lifting my chin. "But I've found you. And you're the only person still awake."

The little man takes off his hat and smooths down the cowlick at the side of his small head, but his curly red hair just springs back skyward when he lowers his hand. "I'm not a person," he corrects. "I'm a bloody leprechaun, for Pete's sake. You'd think you've never traveled before. Never laid eyes on a charming fellow such as myself."

I clear my throat, picking at the thread along my wrist. "My apologies, sir."

"And I'm still awake," he continues sharply, hooking his thumbs into his vest pockets, "because I'm clever, and I know where to hide so the Sandman can't catch me."

Sandman. The word clinks and rattles against my linen skull. I think of the tiny white flecks of sand covering the inhabitants of every town I've visited. "The Sandman?"

The leprechaun stuffs his hat back atop his head, over the unruly cowlick. "For a giant, you don't know much of anything, do you?"

I consider telling him that I'm not a giant, but in fact a rag doll, but I suspect the point will be lost on him.

"The Sandman has put everyone to sleep," the leprechaun says, tapping a finger to the side of his skull. "And now they won't wake up."

I feel my doll eyes go wide, the weight in my chest dropping into my stomach. "I opened a doorway with a moon carved into the front—" I say in a rush, the words tumbling out so quick I hardly hear them myself. "I didn't know what it was, but I think he—" My voice breaks off again. I swallow. "The *Sandman* came from inside it. And now he's loose in our towns and I need to stop him."

The leprechaun stares up at me, his mouth forming a tight little frown. "You opened a door into one of the ancient realms?"

I squeeze my hands together, then release them. A memory surfaces, an old one, from when I still lived with Dr. Finkelstein. He kept a book in his lab, the pages torn and waxy, and inside were stories, folktales about ancient realms that had been forgotten, doorways that had been lost with time. I remember thumbing through the pages, curious about the fables told within it, my eyes absorbing the words as quickly as they could. But before I could get through more than a few pages, Dr. Finkelstein snapped the book from my hands. *This book is not for you, Sally*, he sneered, placing it on his lap as he wheeled away down the dark corridor of the lab. *Your time is better spent cooking me dinner than having your nose in books.* Later, when I tried to ask him about the ancient realms, he shot me a glaring look and sent me to my room.

And now I have opened one.

"It was an accident," I mutter, as if to convince myself, to dull the expanding pain. "But it's not just my town," I continue. "It's all the holiday towns—everyone is asleep. You have to help me stop him."

The little man makes a *snort* sound through his nose, like he's tiring of our conversation, of this unwanted interruption. "*You* let him out," he says with a sharp upturn of his mouth. "Now *you* have to put him back."

"But I don't know how."

"Neither do I." He waves his hand in the air. "The ancient realms were around long before our holidays ever existed."

I shake my head at him, heat burning behind my eyes. "But we have to wake everyone up, or the human world will never have another holiday again." *And I'll lose Jack ... the only one I've ever loved.* "If we don't stop the Sandman, St. Patrick's Day won't happen, either," I say, sounding desperate, a scratching at my rib cage. "And you'll be all alone here ... forever."

The little man steps toward me, raising one of his red scraggly eyebrows, golden eyes shimmering wildly like I have stirred up some hidden part of him. "Then you have to go into his realm," he replies bluntly. "Into Dream Town. Surely someone there knows how to bring the Sandman back to where he belongs."

I shake my head, turning the name over in my mind: Dream Town. The moon-carved doorway, the heady scents that emerged from the tree, they lead to a place called Dream Town. "But what if there are others like him? What if I fall asleep as soon as I step through the doorway? I don't know what's on the other side."

A soft wind stirs up from the trees, and a few raindrops begin to fall from the sky. "Not my problem," the little man spits.

Weight collects against my eyelids again, desperation and fear and doubt. "Will you come with me?" I ask, I plead. He doesn't seem at all like an agreeable traveling companion—he's short-tempered and preoccupied—but I don't want to do this alone. I don't want to go into a town I might not return from.

He lets out a curt little laugh. "I have better things to do," he replies swiftly. "I'm not going anywhere until I find my pot of gold."

"You can look for it when we get back," I suggest, bending low so my gaze meets his, looking him squarely in his beautiful, golden eyes. "I'm sure it's not going anywhere."

For a moment, his features seem to soften. A look of pity cuts into his eyes, like he actually feels sorry for me . . . and maybe it will be enough to convince him to come with me. *Can't let this poor rag doll go wandering off into some dangerous world on her own. Better go with her.*

But then his eyes flash away, over my shoulder. "There!" he exclaims. "That sneaky rainbow."

In the distance, through the soft haze of raindrops, I can just make out the multicolored ribbons of light forming an arched rainbow in the sky. But the place where it meets the ground is hidden beyond a clot of evergreen trees.

"I must be off," he says bluntly, tipping his hat at me. He starts to turn away, then stops, scratching at his beard, considering something, before bending low in the grass and plucking something from the soil. He holds it out in his palm. "Good luck, giant," he says, nodding.

In his palm rests a tiny green leaf.

"It's a four-leaf clover," he explains with a wink. "And one that's been plucked from inside St. Patrick Town is particularly lucky."

I take the green clover from his palm and hold it up to the clouded sky, marveling at its four perfectly rounded leaves. It smells of soil and rain, resting delicately between my fingertips. And it looks just like the clover on the doorway into this realm.

"Thank you," I say to him, but when I glance up, he's already vanished into the thick green spruce trees and falling raindrops.

11

It's nearly evening when I step through the doorway into Halloween Town once more, back to the place where I uncovered the door into an ancient realm—into *Dream Town*.

The sun—a waxen pumpkin—gleams dull and flat on the horizon, hovering just beyond the spiny trees. The air is quiet, and for a moment I think maybe I could pass back through the woods, across the borders of town to my home. I could see Jack, maybe for the last time, before I do the thing I'm about to do. I could run my fingertips along his cold cheeks, whisper his name and tell him I'm sorry, in case I don't return.

But between the stirring of leaves, the wind through the autumn birch trees brings the soft hiss of a voice in the distance—a voice that doesn't belong.

The *Sandman* is still in Halloween Town.

He hums his pensive lullaby, searching for me in shadows and dark corners, trying to beckon me out. He must sense that someone is still awake, someone he hasn't yet found—*me*. Just like Sandy Claws knows which children have been naughty or nice, and Jack knows which children are afraid of black widow spiders and which are terrified of moon-howling werewolves, the Sandman must know who hasn't yet fallen asleep.

I can't risk going back into town.

So instead, I tread deeper into the forest, to the thicket of vines where the newly discovered tree still stands partially hidden. I pull away the dead branches I had used to block the doorway—to prevent anything else from slithering out into our town.

But now *I* will be the thing to slip through a doorway uninvited.

A cold nervous twitch runs down my seamed spine. The fear like salt on a fresh wound, making me want to recoil, to slink back from the doorway and hide in the dark like a coward. I think of the old abandoned well just past Lock, Shock, and Barrel's tree house: I could climb down inside and hide among abandoned cobwebs and forgotten coins from those whose nightmares were never granted. I could stay there and wait. Days would pass, months maybe.

Jack and the others would sleep. And I would be safe and hidden.

At one time, I had thought myself brave—a girl who could surely slay monsters if given the chance, because I am a monster myself. Created by a madman. Living among ghouls and ghosts and grim reapers.

But now I wonder if I'm the wrong heroine for this story. After all, I left a door open into another realm—a dangerous realm. I was heedless, impetuous. I haven't only ruined Halloween, and all the other holidays; I have destroyed the life I could have had with Jack, before it barely began.

The guilt is a double-edged dagger, twisting inside me, breaking threads and tearing me apart.

Can the fool of a story also be the hero?

Doubtful.

But I have loved Jack for too long to let him be fated to a life worse than death. A life spent in a nightmare he can't wake from. I would cross a thousand thresholds into a thousand different worlds for him.

I step closer to the door, fingers reaching for the dark, silver knob.

In the distance, a low hum rises up over the treetops. The Sandman isn't far away now, crooning his drowsy tune, searching, *searching*.

If I don't go now, I'll lose my nerve.

I pull open the small door with the waning moon etched into the wood, feeling the same heavy-eyed lull as the first time I found the door.

I close my eyes and hold my breath, bracing myself for whatever waits on the other side, then

step through the doorway, into a realm the leprechaun called Dream Town.

I plummet through the doorway, landing seconds
later onto an oddly soft, fleecy ground.

It takes a moment for my eyes to adjust—the sky
not quite daylight, not quite night. Somewhere in
between. Above me, tall, lazy trees sway in the
breeze, sagging branches dotted with tiny white
flowers—their fragrance like Swamp Gray tea,
their motion gentle and melodic. I pull the warm
evening air into my lungs, and find myself staring up through their limbs, a calm buzzing in the
base of my skull. The anxiousness I had felt just
before stepping through the doorway has slipped
away like a spring storm, and I feel like I could
coil myself into a shell beneath this grove of trees
and sink into a half-waking daydream. That easy
kind of sleep, eyes still open, watching the silken
breeze push cottony clouds across the skyline.

But I shake off the sensation, rubbing at my
eyes.

I need to stay awake. And I need to keep moving.

The path out of the woods is wide and winding, the air cast in a kind of permanent twilight, a drowsy, dusky quality, while the moon sits full and heavy in the sky. A bloated orb—meant to soothe the weary, seduce them into slumber. Beside the path is a meandering, babbling creek; despite the gentle hush as water spills over rocks, I move cautiously down the path, wary of anything that might appear without warning. This town might be populated with Sandman creatures—hundreds of them lying in wait, sand clutched in their fists, eyes dark and cloying and malevolent.

But the forest is mostly still. Docile-seeming.

Yet I trust none of it.

I peer over my shoulder, charting my way back through the woods in case I need to run, head thumping with fear and adrenaline; I don't want to get lost. Or trapped.

Finally, I reach the edge of the forest and step out into a clearing.

At first, I think it's a meadow, tall grass shushing in the wind. But as I squint through the dusk light, I realize they're fields—rows of perfectly spaced crops, reminiscent of the landscape I saw in Thanksgiving Town.

Only here, instead of corn and pumpkins, the fields are thick with lavender; I can smell its calming, inviting scent hanging in the air.

And startlingly, *impossibly*, there are people in the fields.

My chest rises into my throat, a dizzying whirl of relief and excitement. I watch as they wander the rows of lavender, kneeling in the soil to harvest the fragrant plants. Some are working quietly, others are humming to themselves, slow melodies that remind me of the Sandman's luring songs back in Halloween Town.

People are still awake here.

Yet I stay in the tree line, hidden by shadows, unsure if I should be afraid. They seem harmless enough, farmers working well into the evening light. Although, *oddly*, instead of straw sun hats and work-worn overalls, every last one of them is wearing pajamas—striped pajamas, footed pajamas, pajamas with fuzzy cotton collars and hoods pulled up over heads—as if they should be settling into bed for the night, except they're out in the fields, cutting lavender from the soil.

They bear no resemblance to the Sandman creature. Their slippered feet are planted firmly in the dirt, not hovering above the ground, and no sand spills from their pockets. They are simply farmers, uninterested in anything other than harvesting their crops.

Slowly, I step free of the darkened forest, and move down toward the fields. They don't seem to notice me, at least not at first, their faces bent toward the rows of plants, songs humming from their throats. But as I make my way down the center row through the fields, I reach a man hoisting up a basket of cut lavender into his arms, wearing pale-blue pajamas with white clouds stitched into the collar, and atop his head, a long sleeping cap with a small bell fastened at the pointed end.

He turns, noticing me, but he only tips his head and smiles—as if I were not a stranger at all—then starts down the path away from me, toting the basket in one hand, and a metal candleholder with a tall candlestick burning brightly in the other, to light his way.

"Sir," I say softly, following him down the path.

He stops, and lifts his sleepy eyes to me once again. "The moon was awake . . ." he says dreamily, as if I asked him a question about the soft moonlight. "And it shone on a lake, like a blue bottle rose that grew by mistake."

I tilt my head, confused. "Excuse me?"

"Nothing but time, in a world made of rhymes," he answers in return.

I clear my throat. "I'm sorry, I don't understand. I'm—I was wondering if you might be able to help me."

The man's eyes settle on me, as if deciphering my words, his mind sorting through some old, dusty language long ago forgotten.

"I've come from one of the holiday realms, Halloween Town," I say carefully, not entirely sure if I can trust this man, if I can trust anything here in this strange world. "It seems I've set loose a creature who I believe came from your world. He's called the Sandman."

The man's eyes skirt away from me at the mention of *the Sandman*, quick like a frightened forest animal.

"He's put everyone in my town to sleep and . . . I'm wondering if you know how to stop him?" I swallow, sensing an itch of unease rising in the man. "Or perhaps wake everyone up?"

The man looks briefly like he's going to say something, a tension along his jaw, eyebrows stuffed close, but instead he promptly blows out the candle in his hand—the features of his face instantly sunk into shadow—then hurries away from me down the path, through the rows of lavender. He doesn't even look back.

I feel the seams at the corners of my mouth tug down, unsure what's just happened.

But a few yards away, down one of the lavender rows, a woman wearing footed pajamas with little peach flowers embroidered along the neckline and a candle burning beside her has lifted her head, and is peering at me.

"Hello," I say gently. "Maybe you can help me—"

But before I can finish, she pulls her woolen sleeping cap down over her ears, and turns back to her work.

Although they seem unflustered by a rag doll in their field, the mention of the name *Sandman*

clearly makes them uneasy, a troubled look
darkening their sleepy eyes. But aside from the
leprechaun, they're the first townspeople I've
found awake in all of the towns and realms.

I lift my gaze. In the distance, beyond the
neatly planted rows of lavender, beyond the sloping field, is a massive stone wall encircling a town.

Dream Town.

The man who spoke to me in riddles is moving
toward it, and I do the same.

The path makes its way down through the fields,
to an arched opening in the enormous stone
wall—at least two stories high—where two large,
heavy-looking wooden doors have been swung
open. At the top of the wall are metal spikes jab-
bing toward the muted sky, and etched into the
soft, pale stone, above the doors, are the words
Dream Town.

My eyes fall to the two men posted on either
side of the gate, both dressed in midnight-blue
pajamas, with long wooden shepherd's staffs at

their sides—the kind used to herd sheep—except they hold them firmly, as if they're weapons. A way to fend off intruders.

This town is not like the others.

Its borders are protected, guarded—keeping something out, or in. And a shiver skips down my threads.

The man ahead of me nods at the two guards, then strides quickly through the open gate, unobstructed.

I expect the two guards to stop me, to ask me who I am and why I'm here—shepherd's staffs thrust forward to block my way—but they only nod and make no motion to prevent me from passing into the town. Again, I'm surprised that no one seems startled by my sudden appearance, a rag doll from another realm. But I follow the man with the basket of lavender through the gates, then stop to look out across the dreamy, twilight-lit town, filled with the murmur of voices, a sound that makes the leaves in my stomach stir just a little, after leaving the tomb-like quiet of all the other towns.

The man with the basket of lavender disappears

down a side street, and I move slowly toward the first row of buildings, the walls smooth and white like clay, with tufts of straw poking out from beneath the roofs. Perched at the corner of a building, the windows pushed open, I can smell the scent of a wood fire and cloves sifting out into the evening air. Signs that people are still awake here, an entire town awake, and I could almost cry.

To my left, a woman and a young girl with freckles along the bridge of her nose, are walking up the street toward me—both wearing matching pajamas the color of fresh mint—and when they're close enough, I speak up from the shadows.

"Hello," I say quietly, not wanting to frighten them.

The woman's eyes lift, a hesitant smile ghosting across her lips.

"I'm looking for someone who might be able to help me."

The woman's smile reaches her eyes, gentle, soft, and the little girl beside her chews on her bottom lip, sliding up onto her tiptoes then back down in her footed pajamas. She's fidgety, and tugs impatiently on her mother's hand.

"I've come from one of the holiday towns," I explain, just as I did to the man in the field. "And I believe I've accidentally set loose a creature from your world."

Her eyebrows lift, mouth pinching flat, before she speaks. "A whispered tale is lost, grown long in the tooth, unless there is a riddle that can speak the truth."

I stare at her for a moment, trying to find meaning in her words. "I'm sorry, I wonder if there's someone who speaks more plainly that I can talk to?"

She doesn't answer me, only continues to stare while the little girl sways forward and back, *forward and back*, like she's on a swing.

I hesitate, unsure if I should say the name aloud, but I don't have a choice. "I think the creature is known as the Sandman," I say almost in a whisper, meeting the woman's eyes. "And I need to stop him."

The little girl stops rocking forward onto her toes, her eyes turning huge, mouth falling open, and the woman squeezes her hand tightly, like she's suddenly afraid to let go. Like they're both afraid of me. The woman shakes her head, panic flaring across her eyes, then she pulls the little girl away, up the street, glancing back at me several times before they both vanish into a building with the slam of a door.

Even if I could understand a word of what they're saying, once I say the Sandman's name, the residents of Dream Town don't stick around long enough for me to get any answers.

The name *Sandman* frightens them. Terror stretching across their faces.

Over my shoulder, I can still see the open gate, and out to the fields and the woods beyond. But I know I can't turn back. *I've come this far.* There must be someone who will help me. Someone I can understand, someone who won't flee when I utter the Sandman's name.

I push away from the corner of the building and start into the heart of Dream Town. I keep to the shadows as much as I can, which isn't hard in a town that's caught in a peculiarly endless dusk. The sun isn't visible in the sky, but an odd, glistening light lingers on the horizon, as if it's just set, or is about to rise. That perfect, magical evening hour.

I pass by cottages with candles glowing in windows, rocking chairs on front porches where people sit with large books on their laps drinking steaming cups of golden milk or tea that smells of chamomile and night jasmine. The entire place feels like a storybook, an old world frozen in time.

Everyone is rosy-cheeked with moon-lidded eyes, wearing soft cotton pajamas and thick woolen socks with long sleeping caps, and some carry candlesticks to light their way. But each person I try to speak with responds with a riddle or rhyme or bedtime story, their voices soft and pausing, as if they're caught in a drowsy in-between state. Not quite awake. Not fully asleep.

Yet the deeper I go into Dream Town, the more I begin to have the peculiar sense that someone is following me.

A tiptoeing chill rises along the seam of my spine. A coldness along my fabric skin.

But each time I spin around, no one is behind me.

Not even a shadow slipping just out of sight.

I try speaking to several more residents, but they all reply in confusing rhymes, and whenever I mention the Sandman, their eyes widen and they hurry away.

Finally, I reach the town center, where park benches line the circular street, adorned with cushions and handmade quilts—places to rest, to take a quick evening nap. Several pajama-wearing residents are dozing quietly, and I wonder if their days are endlessly interwoven with naps, and cups of tea by candlelight, and bedtime stories.

Across the town center stands a large stone building, several stories high, with a carved wooden sign that reads LULLABY LIBRARY above the two tall doors gleaming in the lamplight.

I make my way through the square, and pause to peer up at the massive building. We have no structures quite so tall or broad in Halloween Town. Even our town hall is half the size. Posted beside the library doors are two men, both holding long wooden shepherd's staffs, just like the men at the outer gate.

Why would anyone need to protect a library?

I sink down onto one of the benches outside

the library, a throbbing at my temples, a worrying ache pulsing behind my eyes. I felt so certain
that once I entered Dream Town, I would either
meet my end—by falling into a deep sleep, or some
other awful demise—or I would find someone who
knew how to stop the Sandman. *But not this.* Not
a town populated by people who talk in circles.
Who I can't understand. Who are so horror-
struck by the mention of the Sandman that they
run in the opposite direction.

I pick at the fraying thread on my wrist, tugging it loose. Nothing is how I thought it would be.

If I can't find a way to bring the Sandman back
to this world where he belongs, I have no other
options. No other towns to visit. This was my last
chance.

I cover my face with my palms, and feel the
wetness staining my fabric, soaking through to
the dead leaves beneath. Maybe there is no saving
Jack. No saving the other holidays; they will all be
fated to sleep for eternity. *On and on, without end.*
And beneath the soot-dark despair and the pain in
my chest, is another feeling, one that has already
been bubbling beneath the surface and now takes

root, weaving itself around my soft fabric bones. *Guilt*. If there is no undoing what I've done, then there is no atonement.

No setting things right.

No amends.

I wanted this, after all. To be alone. To be anything other than a queen. And now I've gotten exactly what I wished for. *And maybe I deserve it.*

The pressing weight of tears finally breaks over my eyelids, and I don't wipe them away. I let myself cry, sinking into the full brick-hard weight of it all. Of what I've done.

This is my fault.

And maybe I'll never see Jack again—not awake, not as the Pumpkin King. He is as good as dead, just like all the others. Corpses sleeping with eyes stuck closed and minds lost to their nightmares.

The hurt burns against my eyes, the pain in my chest so deep and jagged I'm certain it will drown me. I slip my hand into the pocket inside my dress, feeling for the small green clover given to me by the leprechaun in St. Patrick Town. He said it would bring me luck, but so far I feel wholly unlucky—nothing is as I'd hoped it would be. Tears soak my cheeks, the loose threads in my stomach knot and churn. But between the sobs, there is a voice.

Small, barely there.

"Miss," the voice says again. "Miss, they've sent for you."

I drop my hands from my face, wiping away the salty sting of tears, and look up to see a small boy wearing moonlight-gray pajamas with rabbit ears stitched into the hood. He smiles up at me, missing one of his front teeth, the tip of his nose a cotton candy pink, like he's just woken from a nap. Which he probably has.

"What did you say?" I ask, certain I misheard him, because it sounded like he spoke in a full sentence. Not obscured by rhymes and riddles.

He steps forward and holds out a tiny folded piece of paper, nodding at me, small eyes blinking. I take it from him and carefully unfold the edges.

Come to the governor's house.

I read it twice more, then fold it closed. "Where is the governor's house?" I ask.

The boy meets my gaze, and says, "I'll show you."

I follow the young boy up the street.

We travel two blocks, until the road abruptly ends, and straight ahead is a white stone house with several low clouds gathered above it. As if the clouds have been hung there on purpose, suspended by string, like a child's mobile above a crib. Or painted on with watercolors and dusty white ink.

On the front door is a plaque: GOVERNOR'S RESIDENCE.

The boy climbs the stone steps up to the front door, and lifts the metal knocker, banging it twice against the wooden door.

A moment later, I can hear footsteps on the other side. Not the hard plodding of boots, but the soft *shush* of socked feet. The door swings open and a tall, narrow man in green-and-blue pajamas, with a clean-shaven face, holding a candle to illuminate the doorway, stands before us.

"Good evening," the man says plainly—his words not guised in a riddle—and I wonder if perhaps this is the common greeting in Dream Town, since the sky seems to always be hovering right at a soft evening hour.

He looks to the boy, then to me, surveying me a moment—eyes twinkling—before he nods and opens the door wide for me to enter. "This way," he instructs.

I step into the house, but the boy doesn't follow. He turns and skips back out into the street, his task completed.

The tall man leads me into a long, narrow sitting room just off the entryway. "Wait here," he says.

This man is clearly a butler or doorman or footman—or whatever they're called in this realm—and not the governor himself.

I stand in the center of the room, my eyes scanning every detail, every vase and picture frame. The room is filled with overstuffed pillows in the corners, thick cotton blankets folded and draped across the backs of couches and poufs and cushions. The floor-to-ceiling windows let in the gloaming evening light, while wax candles flicker from the round side tables and atop stacks of books. Above me, the ceiling is painted with a nighttime scene: hundreds of tiny stars and constellations against a deep, river-blue background. It's the perfect room to take an evening nap, just before you settle in for a full night's sleep. I walk to the center of the room and read the spines of several books on the coffee table, picking them up and caressing their covers: They are all bedtime stories, poetry collections, and ancient fairy tales.

"Well, hello." A deep, baritone voice speaks behind me.

I whip around, startled, dropping the book I had been holding onto the floor with a thud.

When my eyes settle on the two figures standing in the doorway, the leaves in my chest wallop into my throat, making it impossible for me to speak. To utter a single word.

They are both rag dolls, just like me.

What an odd thing: to spend your life feeling wholly rare, unusual and strange. To assume there is no one else like you in the entire, endless, known universe. Only to realize, in one stark thunderbolt moment, that you are *not* the only one.

The man and woman peer back at me across the long sitting room, nearly identical rag doll seams along their cheekbones. But where the man has a seam down the center of his chin, the woman instead has a blue-thread seam above her right eye, carefully stitched by a practiced hand. Her hair is long and stick-straight and bloodred, while the man's is a wavy chestnut brown, combed carefully to one side. Just like the people in the fields, and those I've seen in town, they wear matching silk pajamas, paired with heavy robes the same color as the night sky painted on the ceiling above us. The man's robe has a crescent moon stitched onto a breast pocket with royal blue thread, while the woman's has tiny yellow stars.

"We are the governors of Dream Town," the man introduces, flashing a look at the woman beside him. There is an easy cadence to his voice, likable, trustworthy, and I'm amazed I can actually understand him; he's speaking in full, clear sentences, not in irksome riddles. He steps farther into the room, walking to one of the upholstered chairs—but he doesn't sit, just continues to watch me. "I'm Albert, and this is my wife, Greta." He clears his throat. "We've heard that you've been asking questions around town. About the Sandman."

He stares at me curiously—perhaps because I look like them, and he is just as astonished by the likeness as I am. *Rag dolls from two different worlds.*

"Yes," I say, a thousand thoughts and questions lodged at the back of my throat, a wave of relief spilling through me: I can understand them, and they can understand me. And they aren't skittering away at the mention of the Sandman. I swallow, slowing my racing thoughts, and begin again. "My name is Sally Skellington. I've come from Halloween Town, where I am the"—I pause, the word sticking on my tongue like sandpaper—"I am the queen. My husband, Jack, is the Pumpkin King." My eyes flash from the man to the woman; there is something strange in their expressions, a flicker of doubt maybe, like they don't believe me. "But something has happened," I go on. "I left the doorway to Dream Town open by mistake, and now everyone is—"

But the woman—Greta—steps forward, eyes glassy, mouth tugging at the corners, like she's trying to piece something together, solve a riddle in the features of my face. "Sally?" she asks, cutting me off mid-sentence. "You said your name is"—her gaze narrows—"Sally?"

My eyes lock on hers, and she crosses the room until she's only a foot away from me, moonlight from the window skipping across the stitched seams of her soft, pale face.

"Yes," I reply. "Sally Skellington."

Greta looks at me like she's heard the name before. Perhaps rumors of a new queen in Halloween Town have passed through the realms. Perhaps this is something that moves by word of mouth, from one town to another.

She lifts her rag doll hand, a stitched line trailing down each of her fingertips, and she touches my long straight hair, running it between her small fingers.

My heart stops beating.

It's not doubt in the features of her face.

It's recognition.

The seam above her eyebrow tugs together, blue threads buckling. A dampness wells against her linen eyelids. "Sally," she says again, touching my cheek with her palm. Fabric to fabric. Skin to skin. "We're your parents."

12

I wake in a bed.

White cotton sheets.

Autumn clouds painted in thin brush-strokes on the ceiling above me.

The room smells like lilacs and dusty, unused spools of thread. Fabric folded and forgotten, left to the moths. I sit up, and my head wobbles. The words find me again, the ones that sent my mind tumbling, that made the room teeter and turned everything suddenly dark: *We're your parents.*

The same tipsy, inside-out and upside-down

dizziness washes over me now, remembering the way she looked at me, like she *knew* me. Like I was hers and she was mine. Like we belonged together, in some faraway forgotten past. In a dream, perhaps. A time that was never quite real. Yet when she looked at me and spoke those words, some part of me wanted to believe her.

I shake my head, and survey the room. It's a perfectly square bedroom, except for a half-moon sitting nook with windows overlooking the semi-dark town—still not quite night, not quite day. A night-light glows near the door, shimmering an amber warmth, and a jewelry box sits on a dresser near a closet—and in some distant cobwebbed corner of my mind, I can picture a tiny doll inside, a yellow-tutu ballerina that twirls on a pedestal, and a metallic tune that plays when the lid is opened. It feels like a memory. Like I've seen this box before. Known it. Touched it.

I shake my head, clearing away the clouded thought. Someone spent a childhood in this room. Read books in the half-moon nook, made wishes on pale starlight and danced finger puppet figures along the wall, slept and dreamed and felt snug in their bed when someone who loved them tucked them in at night.

But it certainly wasn't me.

And yet, still, the room feels faraway familiar.

Wrongly familiar. And also, somehow, impossibly right.

A gentle knock raps against the bedroom door, and then it creaks open. Greta—the woman who touched my face with her soft fingertips—pokes her head through the opening. "Sally?" she asks quietly, carefully. "Are you awake?"

"Yes," I answer, my voice a childlike whisper in my throat. Caught and strangled.

She steps into the room, hands rubbing together, eyes half-moon lidded, and she stares at me as if *I* might only be a dream. A thing she has wished for, but can't possibly be real. "I think we gave you quite a shock," she says nervously, casting her eyes away, like she doesn't know where to direct her gaze. Like I will vanish if she looks at me too long, merely a bit of morning mist hovering above a swamp, something that will break apart when sunlight reaches me. "But you have given us quite a shock, too, appearing after all these years."

I swing my legs over the edge of the bed, my head still seesawing. "How is it—" I stop myself, start again. "I don't understand." I shake my head and look up at Greta, searching the seams of her face. "I'm afraid you can't be my parents," I tell her. *It's impossible. A story that's surely all jumbled up and spit out wrong.*

She blows out a long exhale, as if she's been holding her breath for far too long—years, decades maybe—and now she can finally breathe. For half a moment, I think she's going to sit on the edge of the bed beside me, touch her hand to my face again like she did in the other room, but she seems to stop herself, her eyes finding me instead. "You were young when you disappeared," she begins, unearthing a story I suspect she hasn't told in a very long time. "Only twelve—a few days after your birthday, actually." She pauses. "You were taken straight from this room, right out through the window." She walks to the windows where a single candle burns brightly, yellow wax dripping down to the windowsill, her face reflecting back in the glass—uneven seams and long cherry-red hair, just like my own.

"But I never had a family," I tell her, shaking my head, still feeling unmoored, like I might tip back to the floor if I tried to stand. "I wasn't born. I was created—built by a scientist named Dr. Finkelstein in a lab. He invented me."

Greta turns to face me. "Our butler, Edwin, saw a pale-skinned man steal you away into the forest that night. The man had small pebble eyes and an oversize head. Is this your Dr. Finkelstein?"

My mouth flattens. *Maybe*, I think. "Was he in a wheelchair?" I ask.

She frowns, then shakes her head. "I don't think so."

My mind races. It sounds like Dr. Finkelstein, but how could it be that he wasn't in a wheelchair? Was he younger then, still able to walk, to sneak into another realm and steal a girl straight from her room? Could Greta's story be true?

"We tried to look for you, we did," she continues. "But the doorways at the grove of trees—the doors to the other towns—were blocked on the other side. We couldn't pass through them. Our town is old, mostly forgotten, and our doorways in the other worlds have been overgrown, lost."

She swallows, crossing her arms. "We never saw you again after that night." A trail of tears leaks from her eyes, staining her cheekbones.

I remember when I found the door to Dream Town, how there had been overgrown vines tangled across the doorway. Maybe the door had been blocked on purpose, by Dr. Finkelstein. Maybe he wanted to make sure the door was never found, and ensure that no one from Dream Town ever slipped through.

Maybe, some part of Greta's story is true.

She walks to the window, gazing past the curtain, then she lifts up something from the windowsill, turning it in her hand. A glass mason jar, empty. "Do you remember this?" she asks, a small quirk at the side of her mouth, a memory.

I shake my head.

"It's the jar where you used to put all of your *angers and sads.*"

I feel my eyebrow lift, my leaves crinkling, too many questions clotting in my mind.

"When you were little," she says, "whenever you were angry or sad about something, you'd whisper it into this jar, then seal the lid tight."

She's smiling fully now, placing the jar back on the windowsill. "You always felt better afterward."

I like the way she looks in the window, muted, pale light across her stitched skin. And I want to believe her words, believe these stories of a childhood I might have had, but none of it feels quite right. Quite like my life. "I don't remember any of that," I answer, scanning the bedroom, looking for anything familiar to remind me of who I might have once been. But only the jewelry box flickers in my mind—something that might have belonged to me once. "If I was twelve when I was taken, I would remember it all, wouldn't I?"

At last, Greta comes to sit on the edge of the bed beside me. And the closeness of her is an odd comfort . . . maybe even *familiar*. Maybe she is the thing I remember, my mind tugging me back to this room, to her. "I don't know," she answers plainly. "I don't know why some memories are lost and others stick like mud inside us. But I remember holding you when you were only a day old. You were so small, your patchwork seams so new and unbroken. Albert kept telling me I needed to let you sleep on your own, in your own crib, in your own room, but I couldn't bear it. I slept with you beside me every night that first year. I named you Sally after my own grandmother, a woman who had your wide, white eyes and who laughed like an owl hooting from the treetops." At this she smiles, a tenderness in her eyes, lashes dipped low.

I touch a hand to the stitching along my chest bone, a peculiar ache fluttering inside me that almost feels like a memory. Solid and real. "I don't understand—" I shake my head, my chest heavy again, the room tipping a little to the left, then right, before I blink and it centers itself. "I was made in a lab," I mutter. "An experiment. Nothing more."

"No," she answers, placing her hand over mine, her voice like a cool winter breeze, as if she could undo what's already been done. "You used to follow me out into the garden." She nods her head, as though the memory was just as clear as if it happened yesterday. "Crawling through the rain-wet soil, pulling up tulip bulbs and chewing on nightshade carrots when you were teething. We baked crescent-moon cookies before bedtime, and I taught you how to sew when you were only two years old. You took to it quickly, always so precise with a needle and thread. You were mending your own seams before you could even walk."

I want to believe her story–that I was a girl with an ordinary childhood. Sucking my fabric thumb and learning to walk and kissed on the forehead by parents who loved me more than anything. A girl who was wanted. A girl who was missed.

Tears begin to break against my eyes, and I can't hold them back. Greta pulls me into her arms, and the scent of her–of lilac linens and warm chamomile honey tea–is like sinking into a warm, summery dream. Like a memory. A tickle in my nose. Even this room, the soft midnight colors, the curve of the mattress beneath me where a girl once slept, feels abnormally, unexpectedly like my own.

The shape of me, carved into the fibers of this bed. A room that remembers me.

Scratched into the fabric of my skull is a word I can hear, one that echoes and grows louder the more I focus on it: *home.*

Maybe this *was* my room. My life.

One I'm afraid to let myself believe might be true.

Another thought occurs to me: perhaps I don't remember this life because Dr. Finkelstein made sure I wouldn't. The endless collection of herbs and potions and foul-smelling chemicals stored in his lab, countless books on all manner of dark things. Perhaps he plucked me from this room, stole me away to Halloween Town, then poisoned me and made me forget. Made me think I was simply a creation. A diagram on a lab wall brought to life by electrodes and wires.

Not a girl born to parents in a world made of dreams.

All this time, I have believed an awful, wretched, unforgivable lie.

But why would Dr. Finkelstein take me away?

I pull myself away from Greta—who might be my *mother*—and in her eyes I try to see myself. A faraway past I had forgotten. But there is too much noise in my skull, threads knotted and frayed.

A moment later, Albert appears in the doorway, knocking quietly, and carrying a cup of steaming tea. "It's wild mint," he says, stepping tentatively into the room, as if it's a place he hasn't been in some time. A room filled with the ghost of the daughter he lost. "You loved mint tea when you were little," he adds, placing the cup on the bedside table.

I smile up at him. "Thank you."

Greta wipes the tears from her cheeks. "You found your way back to us," she says softly.

Albert touches her shoulder, and there are tears in his eyes, too. A thousand sleepless nights when he thought he'd never see his daughter again. When he believed *I* was lost for good.

"We have so much time to make up," Greta says, her cheeks lifting, a warmth surfacing in her eyes. "So many things to discuss."

But hearing her say the word *time* sends a spark like a knife through my chest. Because I'm certain I've already wasted too much of it. "I came here because something bad has happened in Halloween Town," I say quickly, needing to tell her everything, needing them to understand. "Everyone is asleep, in all of the holiday towns, and it's my fault." I swallow down the painful sob catching in the back of my throat, the panic finding me again, even in the quiet of this room. "I need your help waking everyone up. I need your help to stop the Sandman."

The seams along Greta's temples tug down just slightly, and her eyes flash to Albert. "It's not that simple," she says. She stands up from the edge of the bed, then holds her hand out to me. "Let us show you Dream Town. It'll help you understand."

13

Together, the three of us leave the house.

A rag doll and the governors of Dream Town, who might be my parents.

Albert and Greta still wear their long robes and silky dark blue pajamas—common attire in Dream Town—and the sky is the same moody, twilight hue as when I first arrived. The moon full and lazy and low.

"Does the sun ever rise here?" I ask.

"My goodness, no," Albert replies, touching the gray stubble on his chin, the five-o'clock shadow

that I suspect is always there. "It would be too difficult to fall asleep if the sun was up. This is the
perfect quality of light for rest." He waves a hand
toward the skyline, at the faint dotting of stars
just beginning to poke out, giving the appearance
of fabric with tiny needle holes allowing the light
to shimmer through. And he's right, it does cast
a dreamy, drowsy light over everything. Always
beckoning you into sleep. Like it would take no
effort at all; a person could drift off while still
standing upright.

"Why is it that I can understand you both, but
everyone else talks in circles?" I ask.

Albert laughs. "You used to talk in riddles,
too, you know, when you were younger. It's good
practice."

"For what?"

"Our role in Dream Town is to help children,
and even adults, sometimes, fall asleep. We whisper bedtime stories and poems into their ears,
easing them into slumber." Albert looks over at
me, cheeks rosy along the seams of his fabric skin,
gray-speckled hair cut short—a man I can almost
recall reading books to me at night, letting me turn

the pages with my small rag doll hands. Or maybe I just want to believe it—imagine a life where he could have been my father, with his gentle eyes and peppermint candies in his pockets, my favorite mint tea before bed, and his hair that smelled a little of tobacco. A father who loved me, taught me about dreams and riddles and didn't lock me in a basement with a cruel, upturned snarl. "You get used to it after a while, talking in riddles, understanding one another. It's become our common language here." Albert smiles at Greta, a shared knowing between them, a hint of joy that I suspect has been lost all these years that their only daughter has been missing.

But again, I push the thought down, still struggling to make sense of it all—that I could be from this place. That I am nothing like what I used to think I was. "We can still talk in the old, flat language when we have to," he goes on. "When we heard there was someone in town asking questions, using the flat language, we had no idea it was you." He wipes quickly at his eyes so I won't see the tears.

We walk past a row of tiny cottages, smoke

spilling from the chimneys, the scent of lavender and sage cookies drifting on the evening air. I breathe it in, letting the sweet scent settle into my soft, stitched bones, letting it remind me of the girl I *might* have been. How this place could have made me something different—a girl who baked sweets by the evening light, instead of stirring poisons to escape a man who kept me prisoner.

I feel a heaviness in my chest, the burden of too many memories that don't quite fit, but before the sting of tears can push against my eyelids, the ground beneath us suddenly begins to shake, jolting my focus back. The vibration rattles the cottage windows, and my legs wobble at the knees. "What's happening?" I ask, eyes darting to the ground, then up to the sky.

Greta grabs my arm, pulling me into a shop doorway, where the window displays long sleeping caps of various sizes and striped, speckled patterns—caps for children with unicorns and multicolored rainbows woven into the fabric, others in simple muted grays with delicate embroidered stars and moons like the ones Greta and Albert wear. While Greta and I are huddled in the doorway, Albert stays at the edge of the sidewalk, a hand shading his eyes as he gazes up the cobblestone street, as if waiting for something.

A second passes, the clamoring, crushing sound grows louder, and then a sudden rush of white appears.

It takes my eyes a moment to distinguish what's happening, to separate the blur of coiled white-woolly fur clotting the street.

Sheep.

I see three dozen at least, thundering up the street toward the town center. Hooves pounding against the cobblestones, hot air gusting from their nostrils.

Dust swirls up from the street, and I squint my eyes closed against the grit, listening to the rumble of their feet echo along the buildings, the crush of at least a hundred sheep all pushed together, until the last of the herd races past, and Greta releases my arm. I let out a breath, wiping at my eyes, and step back out onto the sidewalk.

"They run amok when they're in Dream Town," Albert remarks, scratching at the back of his head. "A nuisance, really. Counting-sheep only behave properly when they're in the human world. This herd is still in training."

Tufts of white wool lie scattered across the street, dirty hoofprints on the cobblestones, and the air still has a thick, musty smell, like mothballs or a damp wool sweater left to dry on a clothesline. Up the street, from where they came, runs a girl in a nightgown, long black braids bouncing over her shoulders, holding a shepherd's staff—just like the guards at the front gate, and in front of the Lullaby Library. Except hers is meant to actually herd sheep.

"Sorry, Governors," she says as she passes by, tipping her head at them. "I promise they're getting better."

They both smile at the girl, an easy kindness in their eyes. "Just keep them out of the streets, will you?" Albert calls after her.

She nods as she hurries after the stomping, snorting herd.

When she's out of sight, I turn to face Greta. "How long have you been the governors of Dream Town?"

Her eyes seem to shimmer, a starry, half-caught-in-a-daydream expression. "Nearly a hundred years," she says gently. "We had hoped you would take over our role once we were too tired to carry on, but then you were gone and ..." Her voice trails away, and I try to imagine the hurt and grief they must have felt all those years ago, suddenly childless. It must have been the worst kind of ache, a hole inside them that was impossible to fill.

But Greta touches my hand, smiling softly, and we continue on up the street.

They take me through a community garden where valerian and night jasmine are blooming wild and fragrant in neat little rows. Greta squeezes my hand, and I know this must be the garden of my childhood, where I tottered among the plants, learning the names of herbs, and the best time to harvest rose petals. Where I must have found my love for things that grow from the soil.

Just beyond the garden is a wood structure that I think is just a large potting shed, or a greenhouse, but they tell me it's a research center where

Dream Town scientists study sleepwalkers—trying to sort out the best way to coax them back to their beds. In a fenced side yard next to the building, several pajama-wearing townspeople are walking around aimlessly, bumping into the low fence, trying to pick up imaginary objects, while two others hold clipboards, scribbling notes and tapping their chins.

Everything in Dream Town, it seems, is about the study, or encouragement, of sleep.

We continue on, making our way back toward the town center, when the hoot of an owl echoes long and lazy through the streets. Several residents walking nearby glance to their wrists, checking their timepieces.

"The clock owl marks every hour in Dream Town," Albert remarks. "It's how we keep track of the time."

"It's a real owl?" I ask.

"Of course. He's a white snowy owl and he perches atop the Lullaby Library—the tallest building in Dream Town—to ensure he can be heard at the farthest ends of town."

A man and woman walk past us, wool knitted

scarves wrapped around their necks, matching fuzzy slippers on their feet. "Governors," they say, nodding at Greta and Albert with genial smiles.

"You're the only rag dolls I've seen in Dream Town," I comment, seeing myself reflected back in the features of their faces—something I've never known until now.

The seams of Albert's mouth lift into a half smile. "There are a few others. Rag dolls like us, and also several Teddy Bears and Floppy-Eared Rabbits. They are all sleep-weavers, but they spend most of their time in the human world, helping lull children to sleep."

"With so many time zones in the human world, there are always children sleeping somewhere," Greta explains. "So we work around the clock, napping when we can."

She looks at me again, like she's looking for the girl I used to be—or the girl I might have been if I had stayed in Dream Town, grown up within its walls. I would already know these things she explains to me now; I might even have been in line to become the governor.

But still, it's difficult for me to imagine any of

it. To picture a life other than the one I've had—to imagine a life where I never would have met Jack. I clear my throat, thinking of him asleep in our room, Zero nervously hovering by his side, keeping hidden, out of sight, while the Sandman moves through our town. I can't waste any more time. "I need you to tell me about the Sandman," I say bluntly. "What is he? How do I stop him?"

Greta's smile fades from her eyes, her gaze skipping to Albert, then she nods and pats my hand. "We'll show you."

She and Albert lead me down a darkened street without candlelight, shadows sunk into every corner, to a stone building set at the edge of town. It's a rather plain structure, gray walls and a gray roof, without windows or a sign announcing its purpose. "What is it?" I ask.

"This is our Dream Sand factory," Albert says, peering up at the two-story building.

Greta keeps my hand in hers, like she won't let me go, not for anything. "Dream Sand is made here, a proprietary blend of stardust, moonbeams, and a pinch of yawns from the yawning tree that grows just outside of town beyond the peat bog."

"But you must be sure never to venture too close to the yawning tree without proper protective wear," Albert interjects, lifting his stitched eyebrows. "The pale blue pollen is very potent, and can cause uncontrollable yawning."

Just hearing him say the word *yawn* causes a series of large yawns to escape my throat, unbidden. And I think of all the sand I saw in Halloween Town, even the other holidays, how it dusted the sleeping bodies of everyone I found. It was made *here*. In this factory, in Dream Town. And just like at the gate, and the library, two guards are posted at the front door, both looking a tad sleepy; one of them even rubs at his eyes and leans against the long shepherd's staff at his side.

"You have to guard the factory?" I ask, my mind churning back to the feeling of Dream Sand when it touched my skin, when the Sandman sent a swirling cloud of it into our bedroom. How it dusted everything, caught in my hair and under my fingernails.

Greta nods. "We have to protect it."

"From who?" My voice cracks, already knowing the answer.

Greta and Albert exchange a quick look. "The Sandman," Greta answers softly, keeping her voice low so no one on the street nearby will hear.

I swallow and my pulse begins to race, the pieces starting to link together. "The front gate of the town had two guards out front, too."

"Yes." Greta's eyes are cold, seams along her neck tugged impossibly tight. "We only open the gate for a few hours every day, so our farmers can harvest the lavender crops. We keep it closed the rest of the time. And locked."

If I had arrived through the grove of trees at any other time, when the gate was closed, I might still be out there, on the other side of the wall. "You keep it closed because of the Sandman," I say, beginning to understand. "You want to keep him out of the town."

We didn't have a wall in Halloween Town to protect ourselves; we didn't know we should be afraid of things that might slither through open doorways.

"The Sandman is in my town," I say, voice like glass, wanting to shatter. "I need your help."

Greta's mouth goes tight, breathing low, and

she nods. "Come," she says. "It's time we take you to the library."

The Lullaby Library casts a long moonlit shadow over the town square. Pale and watery.

At the wide double doors, we step past the two guards, and are enveloped by the echoey expanse of the library—a massive space that stands three floors high, with four winding staircases in each corner, and a walkway rimming the floors above us. Every wall is lined with bookshelves, and dozens of couches and settees are scattered throughout the main floor. The entire library is lit purely by candlelight, giving it a shimmery, lost-in-a-labyrinth-of-books quality.

Jack would have loved this library; I can imagine him meandering the rows of books, long bony fingers touching the spines of each tome, eyes gleaming with fascination. I feel a pang at the thought, worried that if I can't find a way to wake him, he might never travel to another realm again; he'll never weave his fingers through mine and recite poems from long-lost books or kiss me in the dark corner of a library like this one.

Greta and Albert lead me across the main floor, where several writers are perched on couches, while others doze quietly with notebooks fanned open in their laps, inky pen marks on their fingertips.

We reach the middle of the library, and I breathe in the heady scent of old paper.

"This is the heart of Dream Town," Greta explains, her eyes skipping around the library. "Our poets write hundreds of lullabies a year in this room, songs and stories and riddles to help children fall asleep. Your father even wrote the first theories about daytime dreaming in this library." She smiles at Albert, a look of pride. "He invented daydreams, you know," she says, looking back to me. "A way for humans to dream up wild, unthinkable things right in the middle of the afternoon, without ever needing to go to sleep."

I think back to my own daydreams, moments when I'd managed to lose myself in thought, especially in my old life: dreaming of a future with

Jack, dreaming of who I might be if I ever escaped Dr. Finkelstein.

Albert's eyes crinkle at the corners, like he's embarrassed, and I try to picture him when he was younger: his now-graying hair once a dark brown, seams taut and smooth, hunched over a notebook, conjuring up new ideas for Dream Town.

"The Sandman was humming lullabies in my town," I say, eyes wide. "Trying to lure me out."

Greta's seamed mouth tightens into a grimace. "We use lullabies to help children drift off to sleep, but the Sandman uses them for something else." She pulls in her bottom lip, like she knows, at last, she must tell me everything, but the words are bitter in her throat. "Long ago, the Sandman was the king of our world. But he was not the kind, benevolent man that the folktales would have you believe."

She moves to a small table stacked with old dusty books, touching the spine of one with her fingertips, the cover all black with no lettering on the front. At first her eyes seem soft, the

book unimportant, but then she begins thumbing through the pages until she finds the one she's
looking for. She glances back at me, gesturing
toward the book. When I peer over her shoulder, a
chill slithers down my too-tight seams. Sketched
onto the open page is a roughly drawn image of
a white-robed, gray-bearded man—the Sandman.

"Is this who you saw in your town?" Greta asks.

A stiffness forms in my throat, but I nod.

She closes the book quickly, letting her fabric
palm linger on the cover. "The Sandman was a
stealer of dreams. . . ." She speaks softly now, so her
voice won't carry across the rows of books. "He
would slip into the human world and put children
to sleep so he could take their dreams. In the old
times, children rarely had dreams, because the
Sandman stole them as soon as they drifted off to
sleep."

Albert shakes his head, a line of tension running down his jaw, his hands sunk into the
pockets of his robe. "He was cruel, and greedy, and
we had to increase production of Dream Sand
just to keep up. He stole millions of dreams every
night." Albert draws in a long breath, as though

the words are hard to say. "We worked night and day, double shifts, and we barely slept. The poets were forced to write lullabies until their fingers bled, until their eyes turned swollen and red, and they could barely see by candlelight."

"It was a dark time in Dream Town," Greta says, touching Albert's arm, a gentle consoling gesture, her eyes soft at the corners. "This lasted for centuries, until a group of us began talking in secret when the Sandman was away in the human world."

"We knew we had to stop him," Albert adds, a grit in his voice.

Someone stands up at the far side of the library, stretches their arms over their head, then walks slowly toward the doors—footsteps echoing up the high walls of the library.

Greta clears her throat, swallows, then starts again. "One night, while the Sandman was in the human world stealing dreams, we began building the wall. We closed the Dream Sand factory for the night, the writers stopped writing sonnets, the farmers came in from the fields, and we all worked together to build a tall stone fortress that encased the entire town." She brushes away a strand of her long red hair, and I notice a stray thread on her wrist—just like mine. A nervous habit we both share. And I wonder: has the loose thread grown more frayed over the years? The worry she felt for her missing daughter, revealed in her unmended seams? "Before the Sandman returned, we closed the gates, locking him out of Dream Town."

I feel the leaves in my chest stirring, imagining how frightened they must have been.

"We banished him to the woods outside of town," she continues, exhaling. "And that's where he's stayed, all these years."

Someone a few tables away snores loudly, muttering in his sleep, before another writer with curly ash-white hair and a moss-green cap elbows him in the shoulder, and the snoring man jerks awake, wiping at his eyes.

"Afterward, the town decided no more kings or queens, and our people elected your mother and me to be the official governors of Dream Town." Albert's eyes stray up to the towering levels of books above us, the library so tall, so expansive, it makes me dizzy each time I tilt my head upward. "He's tried to break through the wall several times, hungry for dreams. But we've managed to keep him out all this time, doomed to wander the forests beyond town." Albert clears his throat, swallows. "Until the doorway into your world was opened, and it gave him a way out. Or rather, a way into somewhere else."

I flinch, knowing that *I* was the one who opened the door, the guilt surfacing again. I remember when I first saw the Sandman, slinking through the shadows, checking those he'd already put to sleep, sweeping through every alley and dark corner of town. "In Halloween Town, the Sandman was floating," I say, bringing my focus back. "He drifted up to our bedroom window and blew sand into our room. Couldn't he simply float over the wall?"

Greta picks at the loose thread at her wrist again, fidgeting. "He can only drift up so high, twenty feet at most, before he's too weighted down from all the sand in his pockets."

"What about the farmers?" I ask. "Couldn't he put them to sleep and take their dreams when they're out in the fields?"

"We are residents of Dream Town," Albert says, speaking softly. "We sleep, certainly; in fact, it's our favorite pastime. But Dream Sand doesn't work on us, so the Sandman cannot put us to sleep and steal our dreams."

A jolt runs through me, remembering back to when I tried to wake Jack, when the Sandman blew a cloud of sand through the open window, coating the floor, my hair, and the hem of my dress. *But I didn't fall asleep.* I touched the sand and wiped it away, but felt no tug into slumber. I'd assumed I had been lucky, or that it just hadn't been enough to knock me unconscious,

But now I understand why.

Now I see the truth.

I am *from* Dream Town.

Dream Sand has no effect on me, because I was born within the borders of this world. I am a girl who was *born*. Not made. Heat swarms behind my eyes, and all at once, I know it's true.

Greta and Albert are my parents.

And I am their daughter.

This is my home.

I want to tumble forward into their arms, feel the relief of them against my cotton and linen fabric—*fabric just like theirs*. But my mind won't let me; it tugs back to Jack and Zero and the others. It's even worse than I'd thought: they aren't simply asleep, rather, lost in a dark, dreamless nothing. The Sandman has ripped their dreams away and taken them for himself.

They are, in every way that matters, dead.

"We have to stop him," I say quickly, leaves clawing up into my throat, the panic rushing over me now. It's no longer simply about saving the other holidays, or even Jack—we have to prevent the Sandman from venturing to the human world, and putting everyone in every town and city and province to sleep. We have to stop him from stealing more dreams.

Before everyone, *everywhere* is asleep.

The owl suddenly hoots again from atop the library, marking that another hour has passed. His cries echo through the tall chamber of the library twelve times. Twelve hoots before it falls quiet.

"It's noon," Greta says, as if she senses the slip-ping of time, the urgency of what must be done.

"Please," I say. "We need to go to Halloween Town. We need to bring the Sandman back here to Dream Town where he belongs."

My mother lets out a deep breath. *Mother*—the word already feels easier in my mind, like it's been planted back where it belongs. Fit perfectly into place.

My father's eyes lower.

"I'm sorry, Sally," my mother says at last. "Your father and I have already decided what needs to be done."

"What do you mean?"

"The Sandman is in your world, in Halloween Town. This is our chance to keep him from ever coming back here."

I shake my head at her. "How?"

Her eyes glimmer with unshed tears, but when she speaks, her voice is firm and true. "We're going to destroy our grove of trees. We're going to ensure he can't ever come back to Dream Town again."

14

"You can't!" I shout.

We're no longer in the library; my parents sensed the fury rising inside me, the pitch of my voice climbing into my throat, and they quickly ushered me back to my childhood home, where others couldn't hear the grating edge in my voice. The anger and fear churning in my stomach.

"It's a sacrifice we must make," Greta—my *mom*—says softly, standing a few paces from me in the long sitting room, candles burning low, the air smelling of night jasmine. "To keep the Sandman from returning to Dream Town. Then we can finally tear down our wall, we won't have to guard the Dream Sand factory, and we can go into the woods again, harvest our crops, all without fear."

"But you won't be fixing anything," I protest, feeling a well of tears gathering against my soft cotton eyelids. "Jack and all the others, everyone in the other holidays will still be asleep."

My father blows out a breath and paces to the fireplace, resting a fabric hand against the wood mantel. "We have to protect the Dream Sand," he says, lifting his eyes to me. "We have to keep the Sandman from ever returning and refilling his pockets."

"But there must be some way of stopping him!" I say, the desperation hanging on each word, my voice rising, teetering, like it's about to splinter apart.

My gaze flashes to my mother, hoping she will agree with me, that she will offer some solution other than destroying the grove of trees—the only doorway back to Halloween Town, and back to Jack. But she shakes her head, eyes rimmed with sadness and regret. "I wish there was. But there's nothing we can do. There's no stopping him, only protecting what's left: our town, the Dream Sand, and those who are still awake. I'm sorry, Sally."

I press my palms to my eyes, holding back the tears. "We can't just cut ourselves off from the other worlds," I say, dropping my hands. "We can't just leave them there . . . asleep."

My mom is worrying her hands into knots, and I fear her seams might start to tug apart if she doesn't stop. "There's no way to wake them. I'm sorry. Their dreams belong to the Sandman now."

The throbbing at my temples is like a drum.

"I'm sorry, Sally," my father says, echoing Mom's words.

I sink onto one of the soft, feathery couches, and press my palms to my fabric knees.

"You opened a doorway into your world," Mom says now. "And the Sandman fled. I'm sorry about what's happened to your town, but you've also saved ours, rid us of the monster we've spent a century fearing. You saved us, Sally." She settles onto the couch beside me, her voice sinking low. "So you see, we have to take this opportunity. We have to keep the Sandman from ever returning."

My father drops his hand from the mantel, and looks at me like a dad who knows he's breaking his daughter's heart. "We don't have a choice, Sally," he agrees. "The Sandman has left Dream Town, and we have to keep him from coming back."

A stiffness forms in my throat. This isn't how I thought it would go. When my parents first stood before me and told me who they were, I felt overcome, dizzy with disbelief, but also something else: I was certain that they would know how to defeat the Sandman, that we would return to Halloween Town together, save Jack, and I would finally know the happily ever after of my own story. Tolling bells and kisses with Jack once he woke up.

I didn't know it would actually mean crushed hope and growing fear and tears breaking against my cheeks. "But Jack and the others, I–I can't just leave them," I say, voice wavering, each word a blade.

"I know you care about them," my mother says now, patting my hand where it rests on my knee, her touch like the petals of peonies, silken, tended to. A touch my skin remembers somehow: hands that braided my hair into long neat plaits down my back, hands that wiped away tears when I tore through one of my seams on the spike of a garden fence. These memories are not clear and precise; they rest like gray clouds on a stormy day, only able to be seen partly before they evaporate. "Halloween Town was never your home," she says gently, creeping closer to the truth. "Dream Town is your home. It always has been."

My father nods, lifting his gaze from the fireplace. "This is where you belong, my dear."

"You have been missing for so many years." My mother squeezes my hand like she's afraid to let go, afraid I'll slip from her grasp all over again. "And we finally have you back. I know it's hard to lose the ones you care about in Halloween Town, but you are safe here. It'll be difficult at first, but

I think you can be happy in Dream Town, among your own people. In a world where you are loved. Where you truly belong."

"I was loved in Halloween Town," I counter. But even as I say it, I'm not entirely sure that's true. Jack loved me, of course. But the others? They hardly noticed me before I married Jack. And now, as queen, I am simply a title, a doll they must dress up and make into something new—shiny and suitable and worthy.

Still, I know they are trying to help me understand; they want this place to feel like home. But my heart is breaking. *I can't let Jack go.*

My mother takes my face in her palms. "We are your family. We have loved you long before you came here, long before you knew who we were. You are not an outsider in Dream Town . . . you're home. *This* is your home."

Her words rattle along every seam, a heavy knowing tiptoeing along my thoughts. *Maybe she's right.* Maybe I never should have lived a life in Halloween Town.

It was the wrong life.

And here, perhaps, I am who I was always meant to be.

I feel dizzy, like my stuffing is spilling out of my seams, like I might faint.

Nothing makes sense. I want to scream or cry or sink onto the floor and let myself unravel until I am nothing more than a pile of threads and used-up fabric squares.

Mom takes me by the hand and leads me down the hall to my old childhood room. "You just need to rest for a while," she says softly, sensing the whirling panic in me, the anger and fear and all of it too much.

I want to resist, tell her that I won't sleep, *I can't.*

But my head is blurred over with too many thoughts, and I crave the softness of the bed that used to be mine, the quietness of a house that has already begun to feel familiar, like a part of it was woven into my fabric flesh all these years, I just didn't know it until now. I remember tiny hands along the walls, skipping in new ballerina shoes, laughing, diving into my bed and nesting under the blankets. It was a good life here, wasn't it? Until Dr. Finkelstein stole it from me.

"I can't abandon Jack," I protest again when we reach my room. But even I can hear the weakness in my voice, as if I am a little girl all over again. As if there is no strength left in my chest.

My mother sighs, mouth drawing into a tensely sewn line. In her face, I try to see myself: her large teacup eyes and long spider-leg lashes, the blue thread knitting her imperfect seams together. The more I watch her, the more I know I am a part of her—made of the same woven fabric. "Just sleep for now," she says gently. "When you wake, everything will feel clearer."

I know she's right. My skin feels too tight, my thoughts darting back and forth like a bat trapped in a cavern. I need to rest. "You'll wait to destroy the grove?" I ask.

She looks to the window across my bedroom, the dusky light making watery shapes through the curtain, then nods.

I lie on the bed that used to be mine.

The indentation in the mattress is much smaller than I am now, my feet reaching the end of the bed frame, but still, the sunken center of the mattress is comforting and safe, in a way that makes tears prick against my eyes. The girl who used to sleep in this bed is no longer the girl I am now. She was taken, given a room inside an observatory, told that she was built instead of born. Lied to.

I wonder if my parents are right. And this is where I belong. This house. *This town.* Although my head thumps with the need to rest, I stare up at the ceiling and the mural of stars and constellations. I can't imagine a life without Jack. But if my father is right, and there's no other option—no way to wake the others, and no way to stop the Sandman—then maybe that life is dead. Ripped away like cobwebs in a winter storm.

Maybe they do need to destroy the grove of trees, to keep what's left here safe.

And *maybe* a life here in Dream Town, without Jack, is better than no life at all.

A sharp pain spikes through my chest, and I push myself up from the bed, walking to the window. The town is quiet, far fewer people strolling the sidewalk; perhaps it's finally *night*, a time when the library closes its doors and everyone collectively rests for a few hours.

I try to imagine a life here in this realm, who I'd be if I'd never left. Maybe I would have fallen in love with a boy who writes lullabies, who spends his days in the library, scribbling down sonnets. "Maybe it wouldn't be so bad," I say quietly to myself.

But anyone I might have met in this other life— anyone who eyed me from across a stack of books, or held my hand, or plucked yellow daffodils from the community garden then left them on my windowsill for me to find in the morning—wouldn't be Jack. My heart could never love them in the same deep, dizzying way.

They would never be enough.

A coldness rises in my throat, that wretched, marrow-deep feeling when you lose the last of your hope. When the dark twists around your spine and leaves nothing else. Even if I went back to Halloween Town, there's nothing left. Only shadows. No Witch Sisters or Vampire Brothers, no ghosts or Wolfman or Mummy Boy. They might as well be dead, corpses left to rot in their nightmares.

This life—here in Dream Town—might be all that's left.

I touch the empty jar resting on the window-sill, the place where Mom said I once kept all my *angers and sads*; I wonder if the jar is big enough to hold the mountain of hurt tucked inside me now. Or if the glass would shatter if I tried.

I don't have time for childish things. So I place the jar back on the sill, fingers trembling, then feel myself sink down to the bedroom floor, tears pushing against my eyelids, making prisms of my vision. I press my palms into my eyes and let myself sob. I allow the sorrow to bury me in its miserable, unbearable weight. I choke on it. I die on it. I feel myself lying on the floor of my bedroom, and I wish I wasn't here at all. I wish I had never fled Halloween Town and gone into the woods, tearing off my Pumpkin Queen dress and crow-feather crown. I wish I had never found the door into Dream Town. I wish I would have stayed with Jack, let the sisters pin their fabric into my flesh and insist I wear the highest of heels. I would have felt trapped by it all, but not nearly as bone-breakingly awful as I do now.

I wish I could undo everything.

Because if this is the final page of my story, the last chapter, I don't think I can bear it.

My eyes blink open, stinging from the salty tears, and I peer across the floor of my bedroom to where a stack of books has been placed under the bed frame. They aren't hidden, just shoved underneath the bed skirt as though they were an afterthought. I imagine my younger self, tasked with cleaning my bedroom, hastily pushing them out of sight.

On hands and knees, I crawl to the bed and pull out the books. There are other things under the bed, too: a knitted doll wearing a crimson dress, the bow in her hair coated in dust; a wooden set of jacks; a fiber jump rope coming undone; and several spools of thread in varying shades of blue: cerulean blue like the sea, sapphire blue like a shimmering stone, a teal blue like the sky after a summer storm. But it's the books that hold my attention, and I sink back onto the floor, wiping the tears from my cheeks.

The titles are all unfamiliar, most of the spines broken, bent wide from too much reading. They are books that have been read and reread, worn down, fingerprint smudges and corners folded.

There are books on *Dream Making for Insomniacs, Sheep Counting 101,* encyclopedias on the methods of sleep, theories around daydreams and naps and sleepwalkers. I pull out a recipe book titled *Sleep Tonics,* filled with recipes for golden milk and warm butterscotch cocoa. There is a book on how to choose the correct pillow firmness for side sleepers and back sleepers and roly-poly tummy sleepers, and a DIY book on constructing your own mattress made of recycled fibers and sheep's wool. And lastly, there is a book titled *The Basics of Slumber: Dream Town Edition.*

This book has been read more than all the

others, nearly every page dog-eared, whole paragraphs underlined. It's a manual, a basic guidebook for the residents of Dream Town.

I skim through chapters on the mineral elements of Dream Sand, the importance of moonlight during sleep, how to keep children from having bad dreams, and finally, how to lull even the most restless humans into slumber—those who prefer drinking coffee after 8:00 p.m., and staring at humming, flickering screens in bed. But my eyes linger on the final sentence of the book, the words cycling over and over in my mind: *Everyone, everywhere, can achieve sleep. Some just need to be shown how.*

I lift my gaze to the window, the evening moonlight glinting against the curtain.

"Maybe I've been thinking about this all wrong," I say out loud. Maybe there is a way to save Jack, and all the others—a way I haven't thought of until now, a way that now seems so obvious, so clear, it's been there all along. The knowledge already inside me.

I push myself up from the floor, still holding the book in my hands, tears drying at the corners of my eyes, adrenaline pulsing through me. I have to find my parents.

But when I rush to the bedroom door, and try to turn the cold, silver doorknob . . . it doesn't move.

I try again. I wiggle the knob. I press my shoulder against the door.

But it won't open.

The door is locked.

15

"Let me out!" I yell.

My soft fists bang against the wood door, helpless, useless.

"Please!" I shriek.

But there are no footsteps down the hall, no rising voices coming to save me. The house feels empty, gone silent as a tomb, quiet as a cellar.

I rush to the window and yank open the curtains wider. At first everything looks as it did moments ago, but then I see them: my parents have left the house, my father's hand on the small of my mother's back, and they're walking down the front steps and out into the street, their robes cinched tight around them. To keep out the chill. And in the dim twilight, I notice several other residents leaving their homes as well, gathering with my parents in the street. Huddled at first, speaking low, before nodding together in some agreement.

All at once, I realize what's happening.

I know where they're going.

I slap my palm against the window; I shout through the glass. But they don't turn; they can't hear me. They're too far away, already moving up the street into the faint, watery twilight, toward the gate at the far end of town.

I drop my hand, knowing. *Knowing.*

And the knowing is a sharp stab of betrayal straight into the center of my already broken heart.

They're going to the grove of trees.

They're going to destroy the doorways.

They lied when they said they'd wait.

Keep your thoughts in your head, where they belong, Dr. Finkelstein used to tell me. He wanted a daughter who kept quiet, who did what she was told. Silent and obedient. But I have never been those things. And I refuse to be that now.

I run back to the door, yanking on the knob, hoping to budge it free, but it doesn't give even an inch. *Trapped, trapped, trapped,* my mind repeats, the walls sinking in around me.

My parents have locked me in my childhood bedroom—just like Dr. Finkelstein used to do—and now they're going to destroy the trees, my only way home, back to Jack and Zero and everyone I know. They knew I'd try to stop them, so they tricked me. They lied.

I press my ear to the door, listening. Maybe Edwin, the butler, is still in the house. I pound against the sturdy wood door, calling out to him. But he doesn't come.

Even if he *can* hear me, he's probably been instructed not to let me out.

I hurry back to the window and try to slide it up in its frame, but it's stuck, rusted into place after too many years spent closed—all the years I was away, when no one lived in this room, never letting in the quiet evening air.

Tears break over my eyelids, dampening my cotton cheeks and clouding my vision.

A deep, churning fear swirls in my gut, leaves twisting themselves together like they're caught in a windstorm. *I have to find a way out of here.* I press my forehead to the glass, the panic like a fist in my throat, but through the blur of tears I see the outline of someone approaching the front of the house. *The boy.* The one who brought me the note when I was slumped outside the library. The boy who led me here, to the governor's house.

I slam my palm against the window, yelling through the glass, to get his attention, but he's already letting himself in through the front door.

I run back to the bedroom door and shout against the wood. I beat my cotton fist so hard my stitches start to tear. "Help!" I yell. "Let me out!"

I think I can just make out the tread of soft

slippers on the wood floor, and then, seconds later, I hear his small voice. "Hello?"

The boy is standing on the other side of the door.

"Please," I say. "Please. Unlock the door."

My face is pressed flat to the door, intent, listening, when suddenly it swings open, and I tumble out into the hallway.

"How'd you get stuck in there?" the boy asks, words slurring against the gap in his front teeth, hair mussed, like he's just woken from a nap.

"They locked me in," I say, the breath heavy in my chest, glancing back at the open bedroom doorway.

The boy's eyebrows screw together, like he doesn't understand what I mean, and I straighten myself up and step back into the bedroom, retrieving the book I found under the bed and tucking it under my arm.

"Why are you here?" I ask the boy, stepping back out into the hall and striding toward the front door.

He pulls on his bottom lip as he quickens his step to keep pace with me. "I run errands for the governors, and I came to tell them that the poets are asking for more candles in the library. And to, um–" He scrapes a hand along his neck. "There's a rumor going around that you're their daughter, the one who vanished all those moons ago." His eyes find mine. "Is it true?"

I exhale through my nostrils, clenching at the back of my jaw. "Yes," I tell him, as we reach the front entryway. "But I'm not staying."

The boy follows me out through the front door, and a listless evening breeze coils around me, the air quiet and calm.

"Why not?" he asks, still standing in the doorway.

"Because I am the queen of Halloween Town," I answer, glancing back at him as I descend the stone steps to the street. "And I'm going back home."

I sprint through the town all the way to the gated wall, past the tall fields of lavender, and into the lulling, softly shadowed woods.

"Wait!" I shout before I've even reached the grove of seven trees, hoping it's not too late. Hoping they will hear my frantic pleas, echoing through the woods.

My lungs are gusting with air, eyes flashing through the dark, until at last I can just make out the silhouettes of several people gathered inside the grove. Some hold candles, illuminating the dim forest, while others are wielding axes—swinging them wide, before driving the blades against the hard wood with a loud *crack* that echoes through the far-reaching forest. The sound is like a knife in my ears.

The leaves in my chest rattle with each inhale as I climb the hill toward the grove, the lost needles in my stomach jab and poke. *Please, please, please,* my head screams. But a half second later, I hear the loud *crash*, the sound of a tree hitting the ground and splintering apart, the vibration shaking the path beneath me.

No, no, no.

"Please stop!" I yell. "Please—"

I sprint up the last rise, reaching the edge of

the grove, and at last see the full width of the trees in the trembling candlelight.

I'm too late.

Minutes too late. Moments too late. A whole lifetime too late.

The grove is gone.

Gone.

Every tree has been severed at its base, chopped clean through, and now all seven trees lie on their sides, toppled over like soldiers slain on a battlefield.

"No!" I run to the tree with the golden pumpkin carved into its bark and drop to my knees, clawing at the door, heaving it open. But when I peer inside, I find only the empty darkness of an ordinary, hollowed-out tree. Pale, soft wood, and a small beetle skittering away from the candlelight.

No threshold that will take me back to Jack. No doorway, no passage to another realm.

It's gone.

A hand touches my shoulder, but I jerk away from it. Mom is standing over me. "You said you'd wait," I snarl up at her, through the knotted pain in my chest.

My father steps forward, his seamed mouth turned down at the corners. "We're sorry, Sally. We had to do it."

"No," I reply. I want to push myself up, but my legs feel too weak, all the strength I felt when I fled my room now gone. "You could have waited. You could have told me the truth instead of locking me in my room."

My mother exhales, tugging on the sleeve of her robe, mouth sunk flat. "We didn't want you to leave us again," she admits, eyes trembling like she might cry, like she too might collapse beside me. "We couldn't bear it if you decided to go back."

My eyes flash to her. "So you destroyed the trees, my only way back home, trapping me here?" Each word feels like cracked glass, shredding me open, snapping each thread one by one. "Without letting me decide for myself?"

The seams tighten across my mother's forehead, and I can see the panic in her eyes–the fear of losing me again. "It was wrong of us," she says so softly, the words nearly drown in her throat.

"But we had to make sure the Sandman couldn't come back. We couldn't waste any more time."

I push myself up from the fallen tree, skin trembling, every part of me feeling cut through. They lied to me, hurt me. Took away everything. I have lost Jack for good, and I want to scream, the hurt bulging behind my eyes. I want to tell them that I hate them, that I'll never forgive them. But all the fury sits planted at the back of my teeth, aching, a vile, wretched feeling. Instead, I hold out the book for Mom to see.

"I found a way to stop the Sandman," I say bluntly, coldness rooted in my eyes.

My father squints over my mother's shoulder, while the others in the group raise their candles toward the book, curious. "How?" my father asks, stitched eyebrows pulled together.

"When I found Jack and the others asleep, I tried to make a potion to wake them up." My voice is so thin, it feels like paper. "But it didn't work." I stare at the faces of my parents, wanting them to see the anger in my eyes. To know what they've done. "But I made the wrong potion, for the wrong purpose." I swallow, waiting for some hint of recognition in their eyes, but their features remain slack, motionless.

"What purpose?" Mom asks.

My eyes slide to the book in my hands: *The Basics of Slumber: Dream Town Edition*. While flipping through its pages, I realized I had been thinking about the Sandman all wrong. I had tried to make a potion to awaken those the Sandman had put to sleep. But I needed to think about it like a rag doll—one who was born and raised in Dream Town, who would have spent her nights in the library, studying the fundamentals of sleep. A girl who would have read this book over and over, until she knew it by heart.

"I didn't need a potion to wake everyone up," I say, breathing, glancing to the fallen trees. "I needed a potion to put the Sandman to sleep."

There is a long silent pause, wind shushing through the trees, candles throwing light across the ground, until finally my father speaks. "But Dream Sand doesn't work on the Sandman. We can't put him to sleep."

I shake my head. "I wouldn't use Dream Sand." My voice is still deep, cutting, because I know it's too late now anyway. "I would have made it using herbs that I grew in Halloween Town. They're stronger than anything you have here, more toxic. They can raise the dead, and put them to sleep, too."

"But how would you know how to make such a thing?" my father asks.

I lift my eyes to him. "I've made many dangerous sleeping potions before." But I don't tell him about the noxious soups I used to make for Dr. Finkelstein, all the mornings I would slip poison into his frog's breath tea, knocking him unconscious long enough that I could escape the lab and go in search of Jack.

The hurt expands inside me like rotting flesh, and I'd do anything to go back there now, to see Jack again.

My mother takes the book from me and runs her palm across the cover. "You think you can put the Sandman to sleep?" She raises an eyebrow.

I don't know if putting the Sandman to sleep will wake the others; I don't know if it will break the deep slumber he has cast them into. But at least it will stop him. And I have to try.

But my father interjects before I can say any of this. "The trees are destroyed. There's no way for her to get to back to her world, even if she wanted to."

My mother ignores him, keeping her eyes on me. "Sally. If you could reach your town, do you think you'd be able to stop the Sandman?"

I swallow and push my shoulders back. "I would try."

My mother glances back at my father, some silent thing passing between them. "The human world," my mother says at last. "You can reach Halloween Town by going through the human world."

I feel my dark pupils narrow on her; the stirring in my stomach falls still. I've never been to the human world—the place Jack visits every autumn on Halloween night, slipping through graveyards and cemeteries and mausoleums. It's how he moves back and forth between our realm and the mortal one.

But I haven't seen a cemetery in Dream Town. Not even a single headstone.

"How do you get to the human world?" I ask.

Mom lowers the book, meeting my gaze. "We'll show you."

The Lullaby Library is quiet, an after-hours kind of silent. No one curled on the love seats writing riddles. Everyone's gone home for the night, to rest their eyes and minds.

Yet we walk in silence down the center of the library, my mind still burning at the thought of what they did: *Destroying the grove, trying to trap me here for good.* It feels as deceitful as Dr. Finkelstein locking me in my room, making me a prisoner. *You are a treacherous, willful girl,* he would say. But is it willful to want freedom? To choose your own way? To risk everything to save the ones you love?

My parents lead me up a set of metal spiral stairs, and at the second floor, we climb up another spiral stairway, then another, until we're perched on the third floor—the highest part of the library.

We move along the walkway beside tall, endless stacks of books, but the titles are unreadable in the dim light—only a few candles still burning on the shelves to light our way. Finally, at the back of the library, we come to a door made of dark cherrywood, with an ornate spiral of nighttime stars etched onto the front, and darkened as if the wood has been burnt by a flame.

"This is our way into the human world," Mom whispers, speaking softly even though there is no one else inside the library. "But if you leave," she adds, "we will still—" She swallows, a heavy darkness in her eyes, then picks at the thread on her wrist. "We have to make sure the Sandman doesn't return. . . . We have to destroy this doorway, too. Close off any chance of him getting back in."

I breathe and the library seems to expand, walls stretching outward, while my thoughts close in around me. "But if you destroy this door, you'll be closed off from everything," I say. "Your Dream Sand, all the lullabies . . . you won't be able to help anyone fall asleep anymore."

"We don't have a choice," my father says, repeating his words from the grove.

I draw in a deep, unsteady breath, and in their eyes I can see how desperately they don't want me to leave. How they'd do almost anything to keep me here, to make me stay. *Even lie.* But I can't stay. I'll sacrifice everything—even this town that was once my home—if it means I might be able to save Jack, see him again, feel his hands against my linen skin.

I'm returning to my world, knowing I'll likely never see my parents again.

Tears form in my father's eyes, his mouth trembling.

"I know Dream Town might be where I belong," I say, wanting my parents to understand why I have to see this through. Why there's no turning back now. "But it will never feel like home without Jack. I have to try to save him. All of them." Even though they have lied to me, hurt me, my heart still feels like it's breaking all over again. I don't want to leave my parents behind—not now that I've finally found them. "He would do the same for me," I say, my voice cracking on the words, mouth trembling.

My mom tugs me into her arms, wet tears and fabric skin made of the same linen and thread. A patchwork pattern that makes us the same. And I let myself cry.

"For so long we never knew what happened to you," she whispers against my cheek. "We worried every day. But finding you now, I realize you are braver than I ever imagined you might be." Her words rupture into a sob, then she takes a ragged breath. "I don't want to lose you again, but I know you need to fight to save the ones you love, and there's nothing more worthy than that."

"Thank you . . . Mom." I say the word out loud for the first time, tears shedding down my face in rivers now. My father folds his arms around us both, and I feel a flicker of doubt. Small, imperceptible, but there just the same. Stabbing at me.

Am I wrong to leave?

I have finally found my family, and now I'm leaving them to go back to a place I might not be able to save. If I can't make a potion strong enough to put the Sandman to sleep, if I can't stop him, if I can't wake the others . . . then what? I'll be trapped in Halloween Town all alone, with no way to return to Dream Town where it's safe.

I will spend the rest of my life hiding from the Sandman.

But this brief, thumbnail-sized thought is quickly replaced by a larger one. The one that overtakes all others.

I was born in Dream Town, but I am also the Pumpkin Queen.

I will fight for Jack. I will fight to set things right.

I pull myself away from my parents' arms, then step forward and open the wood doorway, a strange, cold hiss wrapping itself around me—the interior dark and shadowed, no light at all.

"When you step inside," my mother instructs from behind me, "you will be taken to a library in the human world."

"Which library?"

"Whichever one you want," my father says behind me. "Think of a town or a place as you step over the threshold, and the doorway will open up into a library there."

My head pounds as the names of towns, cities, locations in the human world skip through my mind, all of the places Jack has described visiting on Halloween night. But how will I choose just one?

"I'll have to find a cemetery," I tell them. "That's how I'll get back to Halloween Town."

"Try to think of a smaller town, then," Mom offers. "So you won't have to search as far."

I nod and take a deep breath, looking back at my parents—both still crying, arms folded around one another. I've found them—but now I'm leaving them behind—and I'll never see them again after this moment. This last goodbye. The burden of what I'm about to do feels almost unbearable, but I hold open the door and suck in a breath.

I smile at my parents one last time, wanting to say something—*one last thing*—but I can't find the right words, good-enough words. My head and my heart are a traitorous, treacherous mess, both wanting different things, both colliding inside me and making it impossible to speak. So I don't.

I love them ... somehow. These two people who I've just met. Fabric scraps and long red hair: we are the same.

But I have to let them go.

I peer into the dark of the doorway, knowing that once I've passed through to the other side, my parents will destroy this door, break it apart, maybe even burn it until there is only ash.

Until there is no magic left inside.

I close my eyes, count to three, then step through the doorway.

16

In Jack's dazzling, wondrous stories of the human world, he often described cities that stretched as far as the eye can see, towering buildings, buses and trains crammed with people traveling from one city to the next, from one country to another. A place thrumming and noisy and endless. It always sounded terrifying to me, a place to easily get lost in, possibly forever.

But when I step through the doorway, it doesn't seem large at all.

Just a library.

Rather ordinary in size, even small, compared to the Lullaby Library. Velvet couches are arranged in perfect formation beside a fireplace, and a few upholstered chairs sit beside a bank of windows— the fabric a tightly woven silk, depicting a scene of meadow flowers and a handsome manor house in the distance. It's well-made fabric I would kill to have for my own flesh. Bookshelves tower above me, with most reaching so far upward that there seems to be no way to retrieve them. Old tomes no longer read, no longer pulled from the shelf.

I walk to the wall of windows and peer out at a green expanse of manicured lawn shimmering beneath the sunlight, with flowering trees in pale white and soft, buttery pink. I have no idea where I am. But from what I can see, the stone building where I stand appears to stretch outward on both sides, massive and sprawling into the garden and beyond. It feels like something I've seen in a story-book. It feels like a castle.

I start to turn away from the window, to head for the nearest door . . . when I hear someone breathing, low and soft.

I'm not alone.

I scan the room, and notice the back of a head resting against one of the upholstered couches, facing away from me. Someone is seated in the room, quiet except for her breathing. Tentatively, I move toward her, unsure how she will react to a rag doll in her library. *Ready to run, to bolt toward the doorway on the far side of the library.* If this was Halloween night, my appearance would be suitable for drawing out screams, but on this average evening, a rag doll is not something that should be seen in the human world.

As I get closer, I notice that she's more slumped than sitting, shoulders dropped, cheekbones slack— and what I see next makes my stomach drop with a painful jolt. My head starts to swim.

A fine layer of white sand covers her short gray hair, still pinned and curled perfectly in place. The sand is scattered at her feet and dusting her pressed and tailored clothes.

She's asleep, just like all the others.

Just like the holiday realms.

The Sandman has already been here . . . to the human world. And my body wants to give out, sink to the floor and press my forehead to the cold wood. *Everyone is asleep.* The small flicker of hope I felt vanishes, blown out like a candle. How long ago was he here? And is he still in the human world . . . a place so vast I can't imagine finding him?

I inch closer to the woman, feeling drawn toward her, pulled. She looks rather serene for someone who's fallen into such a sudden, baleful slumber. Around her neck rests a delicate row of pearls, in her ears, a matching pair of earrings. She is polished, courtly, a woman who surely doesn't comb her own hair or place her own shoes on her feet. A woman who is tended to.

I know I should leave, find the closest cemetery and slip back into Halloween Town—I need to get back, make the potion, and then somehow find the Sandman—but I feel captivated by this woman, intrigued by her neatly arranged dress and this seemingly private room where she sits. I walk to a desk near a window, touching the small stack of books—poetry volumes, ancient literature, books on government and royal standards. I turn in a circle, and my eyes settle on a painting over the fireplace. I move closer, tiptoeing even though there is surely no one awake who might hear me and come to investigate my intrusion.

The painting, I realize, is a portrait of the same woman who is asleep on the couch. She's a few years younger in the image, her speckled-gray hair curled around her ears, and she's wearing a long white-and-gold dress with a sash, and several odd things pinned to it—squares of paper and silver tokens. And on her head sits a crown—silver and ornate and shimmering.

At the bottom of the gilded frame is a bronze plaque with the words: QUEEN ELIZABETH II.

I glance back at the woman, and then around the library.

Before I left Dream Town, my father said I needed to think of the name of a town when I passed through the doorway, but the only word that kept repeating in my mind, the word I still can't seem to shake, was *queen*.

And now it seems, I have arrived in the library of a queen.

While the queen herself sleeps only a foot away.

I walk to her and settle carefully onto the

cushions beside her. I feel curiously drawn to her, the elegant tilt of her chin—even while she sleeps—and the graceful, delicate fold of her hands in her lap, a wedding ring on her left hand. Time stretches out around me, the urgency with which I entered her library briefly dulled.

I peer up at the painting again, and although she doesn't appear quite as fussed-over in real life as she does in the portrait, there is still *something* about her. A magnificence that cannot be measured in the weight of the silk that makes up her gowns, or the jewels draped over her pale human skin. She has the *soul* of a queen, sleeping or not. Adorned and bejeweled or not. It's in the breath that rests in her delicate lungs, the refined features of her face, the firmness in her jaw. She is dignified and stately and noble.

I suppose some people are just born with it in their veins.

But I wasn't.

My queenly title came later. Burdened and heavy and unnatural.

Yet my gaze keeps flicking from the painting and back to her, trying to see something. The in-between part of her, that hidden, *true* part. If only she was awake, I could ask her what it feels like to be a queen in the human world. If she feels suffocated at times by her duties, by the glances and stares she receives from the people of her town; if they have ever looked at her as though she's not quite good enough. I would ask her how long she has been queen, and if she wanted this role or if it was handed to her—forced upon her. I want to know the story of her life.

On the oval-shaped coffee table sits a pot of tea, gone cold, a delicate, daisy-studded teacup beside it, the liquid inside half-consumed. The scent is faintly of lemon. It feels like such a normal thing—to be sitting and drinking tea in a library. Pleasingly normal.

She is a woman who could just as easily be a grandmother, who might bake cookies on Saturday mornings and knit scarves for her grandchildren well into the night. Maybe she is all of these things, and *also* a queen. Maybe she can be both.

A queen with a crown, her portrait hung on the wall.

And a grandmother.

And a woman.

Maybe, *maybe*, I can be both, too. A rag doll *and* a Pumpkin Queen. In control of her own life, her own royal title. A queen who doesn't allow the sovereignty to overshadow the rag doll she's always been. I place my soft hand against the queen's. Only gently, for fear I'm not supposed to. But I want to feel the humanness of her skin, to know that she is *real*, and that even a queen has blood running through her veins like any other mortal. A queen touching another queen's hand.

I swear I can feel the nobility of her through her skin—like a golden, shimmery light. The strength of a woman who has seen many things, overcome much in her long life. A woman who was meant for this role.

Yet I'm certain that not every princess or duchess or queen has felt like they belonged. Not every crown worn inside this library, this castle, has felt steady or sure on the heads where they sat. Perhaps the crown has sat heavier on some heads than on others. Threatening to break them, or reshape them into something else. Something even mightier.

I swallow down everything rumbling inside me: the hurt and the fear and the gut-churning doubt. And I wonder if I can be shaped into something stronger, too. Sturdier, resilient. Even if my seams can be broken, that doesn't mean *I* will be.

I draw my hand away, allowing myself to smile just a little.

"Thank you," I whisper to this queen—Queen Elizabeth II, of some realm, some city within the human world. I stand up from the couch, looking back at her one last time. If I can save Jack and the others, I will also be saving her. A queen who will never know that she met the Pumpkin Queen while she slept, or was brought back from a dreamless slumber because of me.

I cross the library to a set of doors, taking in a deep breath, stirring the leaves in my chest, and step out into a grand hall inside of a castle much larger than I was expecting.

This woman is not just any queen.

She might be *the* queen.

It's raining outside when I finally make my way through the labyrinth halls of the castle, and step out into the dreary day. I leave through a tall metal gate, past two ornately dressed guards lying on the ground, one curled up like a child, the other with arms spread wide to the overcast sky, both sound asleep.

Ahead of me, a wide walkway is framed by green grass and perfectly spaced trees. And scattered as far as I can see, are humans dozing on park benches, on sidewalks, or in the neatly trimmed grass. All of them dropped cold where they stood. Sand strewn over everything, filtering down from tree boughs, clinging to the skin of every person I see.

The Sandman has already been here.

Everywhere.

And if I can't stop him, they will all stay asleep . . . forever.

I bite down on the ache inside me, the fear and gravity of what I must do. And what will happen if I don't—if I fail. The burden rests solely on me.

I release the thread at my wrist, stepping past the gate—I have to find a way out of the human world—and I break into a run, sprinting down the long thoroughfare, past sleeping bodies, until the lawn gives way to buildings built much too close together. I have to find a cemetery or a graveyard. Even a church will do if someone has been buried there. I turn onto a wide concrete road, and keep running.

Jack was right when he said the human towns are unlike any in the holiday realms; they are much, *much* larger. But as I make my way up the streets, searching for anything resembling hallowed land—a place where humans have buried their dead—everything is eerily quiet. Only the sound of the birds and the soft rain against the street.

I press on, searching down rows of brick homes stacked side by side, shops with OPEN signs in their windows, but everyone asleep inside. When I reach a corner, or a side street, I turn left, and then right. I have no idea where I am. I spot a library set back from the street, but I know that I couldn't return to Dream Town now—even if I wanted to—the doorway back into the Lullaby Library has surely been destroyed. No going back, only forward.

I pass a market, a hair salon, a clothing store with an array of oversized handbags and colorful shoes and sparkly necklaces in the window display. Still, everywhere, people are sleeping: snoring, clutching paper cups of coffee spilled onto the ground, some sitting in automobiles slumped against steering wheels. The city sits entombed in silence.

No car horns or wailing babies or the thrum of human activity.

Nothing.

At last, as the light in the sky begins to dim— the doubt growing larger inside me—I finally spot an old stone archway, a high wall, and through it . . . I find what I've been looking for.

Relief shudders through me, and I gulp down a breath as I step through the archway that reads BROMPTON CEMETERY, and into an expanse of land dotted with carved stones.

A graveyard.

It's the largest cemetery I've ever seen—a place Jack would surely love.

A long rectangle of green lawn lined with rows and rows of old, moss-coated and weather-worn gravestones. Rain pounds the earth, and the cold tickle of air against my neck reminds me of the cemetery in Halloween Town. A feeling that exists in every cemetery, it seems. That hint of death. Of sorrow. Of lives brought to an end. But I don't have to go far before I find a small stone structure, an ornate mausoleum with spires along the roofline and a copper door, tarnished green from the rain. A tomb where the dead are placed to rest.

I glance up the path, the cemetery glistening in the wet air. I have passed through many realms, all the way into the human world to a city made strangely silent, and now this mausoleum is my way home.

My way back to Jack.

I feel the leaves stir in my chest, knowing how close I am to finally seeing him again, and I pull open the door into the tomb—the cold inside like winter air, the dark absolute.

I swallow down the anxiety and fear beating against my tired seams, and I step through the mausoleum door into the cold, cold dark, thinking of *home.*

CHAPTER SIXTEEN

And when I step out the other side, through the dim, lightless burial chamber, I emerge into a familiar cemetery.

I am back in Halloween Town.

17

Halloween Town is quiet. The wrong kind of quiet.

The dark corners and shadowed alleys where grim, monstrous things usually lurk have all gone still.

Dead leaves thump in my chest, beating in my ears, and I move quietly through the cemetery. For a moment, I think the Sandman is gone—traveled to one of the other holiday towns or still making his way through the human world—but as I creep closer through the shadows at the outer edge of town, I hear it.

A low, humming croon.

A whispered lull, like water and woodsmoke, coiling, creeping into my ears.

The Sandman is here.

Searching, searching. For me. A chill travels down my seams, landing in my toes. He's looking for me, hunting me.

But I have come back, in search of *him*.

I can't tell where he is, his voice echoing over rooftops, so I keep to the dark shadows, sprinting from one to another like a spider afraid of daylight. Now that I know the truth—that I was born in Dream Town—I know his Dream Sand won't work on me. But I also don't know how deep his cruelty runs. If he discovers me, and realizes he's unable to put me to sleep, what other awful, cold-blooded thing might he do? Maybe he'll rip me apart at the seams, stitch by stitch, until I am only a pile of dead leaves and shredded fabric. Nothing left to put back together.

So I stay hidden, careful, tiptoeing through

the dark. I make my way to the garden behind Dr. Finkelstein's lab where I quickly gather the herbs I'll need: deadly nightshade, black valerian root, foxglove, and a pinch of corpse flower—meant to mimic the effects of the dead.

I hope it will be enough.

It has to be enough.

I sneak down the alley behind Dr. Finkelstein's lab, black shoes making the softest sound against the stone, when I hear the Sandman's humming song—sounding closer than before—a slow, ghostly lullaby vibrating down the darkened streets.

Silently, breath held tight in my linen chest, I slink along the perimeter of town, pausing beside the Witch Sisters' Apothecary, listening. A second passes, then another. I clutch the herbs in my hands, trying not to make a sound.

But the Sandman has fallen quiet.

Perhaps he's moved to the far edge of town, searching the woods. I step into the open, ready to dart the last few yards to the gate, and into our home, when a shadow flashes overhead.

Dark and horrible.

Him.

I nearly drop the herbs, scrambling back out of sight—back pressed to the stone wall, needles stabbing at my gut, the fear weaving up and down every inch of my threaded seams.

But after a moment, the Sandman's shadow slips past the alleyway, and moves farther back into town. Into the dark. *He didn't see me.* And this is my chance. I push myself away from the wall and sprint the last several yards to the gate, taking the steps two at a time, scrambling into our house.

Inside, I yank the door closed and slide the lock into place.

Gasping, gasping, my lungs screaming in my chest, ears ringing.

But I made it.

I climb the spiral stairs up to our room, clutching the herbs in one hand, the threads along my chest humming, fingers trembling, and when I step into the bedroom, I find Jack right where I left him: asleep in our bed.

Tears trail down my face. *He's still here.* And he's still asleep.

I step farther into the room, about to cross to

the bed, when a shadow slips out from the closet, a deep growl echoing across the room.

Zero drifts into the faint moonlight cast through the window, his teeth bared, a rumble in his chest—ready to protect Jack no matter what. But when he sees me, his ears suddenly drop, and he rushes toward me, burying his head against my chest. "I'm okay," I whisper into his fur, folding my arms around him. "I made it back."

He makes a whimpering sound, nudging in closer to my neck.

"Thank you for staying behind," I say to him. "For watching Jack."

Tears fall from my chin. I am unable to hold them back. I've felt so alone since leaving Halloween Town, and now—being back in my home, my bedroom—and finding Zero still awake, has broken open a part of me. I feel a strange relief, woven together with the nagging prick of fear.

Zero drifts back from me, his dog eyes damp at the corners, and I stroke my hands down his fur one last time before I hurry across the room to Jack. I drop the herbs onto the nightstand and climb onto the quilt beside him. My body heaves, my eyes burn with tears, and I rest my head against his chest, listening to the hollow echo. I close my eyes, and for a moment I wish I was asleep just like him, lying side by side, each trapped in our own dreamless darkness.

But Zero moves close and nudges his nose against my cheek, eyes blinking. Maybe he knows I can't stay here, I can't curl myself up with Jack and rest. I have to keep moving. The longer I stay in one spot, the more likely the Sandman will discover me.

I run my fingertip along Jack's cheekbone. "I'm going to try," I whisper, even though he can't hear me. And I place my mouth on his, kissing his sleeping lips. "I'll make this right."

Using a bit of string from the spool in my pocket, I tie my hair back into a ponytail—out of the way while I work—then hurry back downstairs to the kitchen. I retrieve a cast-iron pot from a hook above the sink, and light a fire, working quickly. I grind up the herbs, then place them into the pot, measuring three times the usual amount. It's enough to put a woodland giant to sleep for an entire year, but I need it to be strong. I will only get one chance for this to work.

I stir the simmering potion until it turns a bright, gruesome red, the same shade as Ruby Valentino's lips. But it's too bright, too obvious.

Then I remember.

I reach into the pocket of my dress, past the spool of thread, to the thing I'm looking for.

When I pull it out, the leaves are slightly flattened, but it's still intact: the four-leaf clover given to me by the leprechaun in St. Patrick Town. He said it would bring me luck. And I need it now. I drop the green clover into the potion, and within seconds, the color turns a vibrant, grassy green—reminding me of the damp meadow in St. Patrick Town, freshly dewed with rain.

The exact shade I need.

Once the brew has boiled down and the scent is so rich and noxious that I feel light-headed, I pour it into a glass jar, stoppering it with a cork.

The potion is ready.

Now to make the decoys.

Back in our bedroom, I pull out the old sewing machine from the closet, and gather the yards of fabric that the Vampire Prince and the Witch Sisters brought over for my absurd queenly wardrobe. I wanted to be rid of it all, hated the feel of the gauzy fabric pinned to my skin, but now it'll be useful.

I tear off odd strips of fabric, and begin sewing them together, pinching my tongue between my teeth while I work, stitching six patchwork dresses that look just like my own, six pairs of arms and legs, six faces and torsos. I work through the night, sweat at my temples, fingertips worked raw.

And when the sun finally breaks over the horizon, streaking a soft, dreamy orange through the windows, I stand from the sewing machine to survey my work—Zero hovering beside me, his head tilted curiously to one side.

Across the wood table, lie six lifeless rag dolls, each wearing a patchwork dress.

With the sun now sitting fat and bright in the sky, there are fewer shadowed places to hide. But I slink through town, tiptoeing quietly along the streets, then pausing at each corner, listening for the Sandman. I can hear him in the distance, never far away.

But I need to keep moving.

I told Zero to stay at the house—with Jack—and now I skirt along the edge of the town square, stopping to position the first doll in the doorway of the Witch Sisters' Apothecary, suspended by string from the doorframe so the wind catches it slightly, stirring the doll's arms and legs as though it's alive.

A decoy.

I hurry to the outer border of town, stringing three more beneath the bare branches of the spiny Howling Trees—magpies cawing at me from the limbs, making too much noise. Once secured, I drag the last two dolls toward the center of town.

There are fewer shadows here to hide beneath, the sun glaring down brightly from above, but I manage to hang one of the decoys in the massive spider's web on the east side of the town square, suspended between two buildings, the fake rag doll's arms clinging to the sticky web. Briefly, the black widow scrambles down from her hidden perch, investigating the lifeless doll. She scurries over it, eyes like domes; then, deciding there is no blood to be drawn from the fake doll, she hurries back up to her corner, tucked safely away where she won't be seen.

Dragging the sixth and final doll, I cross the town square, when I hear the Sandman's lullaby. But it's different this time, slower, a tiptoe over each rhymed word.

And I realize: he's located the first doll hanging from one of the Howling Trees.

He thinks he's found me.

There is a sudden quiet, a lull in his song, followed by a swift rustling. I can't see him beyond the row of black stone buildings, but I suspect he's blowing sand into the fake rag doll's eyes, hoping she'll fall into a bottomless sleep. Another moment of quiet. No lullaby, no humming. And then the echoing crack of branches, like he's ripped the doll from the tree and tossed it to the ground.

His song resumes, followed again by silence. He's found another doll.

I need to hurry.

I reach the Town Hall and place the last rag doll on the steps, bending her legs at the knees and folding her arms in her lap, to make her appear as though she's quietly enjoying the late morning sunlight, while the Mayor snores beside her.

The sound of more snapping tree branches echoes through the town, the crack and splintering of wood: he's found the other two dolls.

With my leaves trembling in my chest, I hurry back toward the fountain.

I'm almost to it, when from the corner of my vision, I catch sight of the Sandman—cloud-tinted robes dragging along the street, gray wispy beard longer than I remember, and a cruel, awful look in his dark-rimmed eyes. He rounds a corner near the Witch Sisters' Apothecary, a slow, winding hiss leaving his lips.

I drop to the ground, the jar of potion nearly slipping free from the pocket of my dress. If the jar broke and spilled the noxious potion at my feet, the fumes might be enough to knock me into a deathly sleep forever. Carefully, I slide the jar back into my pocket, then scramble beside the low brick wall that encircles the town center. It's hardly a hiding place. But I try to make myself small, coiled into a ball—just a heap of fabric, nothing more.

The Sandman spots the fourth decoy in the doorway of the Witch Sisters' shop and quickly blows a handful of sand into its eyes. But the doll just hangs there, moving gently in the morning breeze. I can see the irritation cut along his forehead, and he rips the doll from the doorway, pulling off its stuffed cotton head and throwing it to the ground. He grips the limp body by one foot, and drags it for several yards, until he notices the fifth doll suspended from the spider's web. He drops the headless doll and darts toward the web. But he doesn't blow sand into its eyes: he stares at it suspiciously, drifting closer to touch one of the rag doll's hands. His mouth seems to lift in a snarl, and he lets the doll's hand fall back into place. He knows it's a fake.

He sees through the trick. And he rips it free from the web, breaking several of the spider's careful strands, then tosses it to the ground.

I waited too long. I should have sprinted to the fountain when I first heard him at the Howling Trees. I should have made more decoys. But it's too late now.

The Sandman turns, scanning the town square, moving slowly—like he senses he's being watched. Something isn't quite right. He spots the last fake Sally perched on the steps of the Town Hall, and he begins moving toward it, but not with the urgency he did when he spotted the others. His gaze darts to his left, the right, and I have to sink farther into the narrow shadow where I'm hidden, tucking my arms and legs close. If he finds me, if he can't put me to sleep like the fake dolls—because his Dream Sand won't work on me—will he rip off my head just like the decoy? Popping seams and broken thread, and my head is no longer attached to my body.

When he's within a few yards of the last doll, I slink one leg out of the shadow, then the other. I risk stepping into the sunlight.

I have to do this quickly. Or not at all.

My heart is a sledgehammer, my throat dry. The

Sandman bends down to examine the fake doll, he pokes it with his white fingertip—suspicious.

This is my chance. I sprint across the open space between the low stone wall and the fountain. The sun glares down at me—the air too quiet, my footsteps too loud. Everything moving in awful slow motion. At the fountain, I collapse down against its stone edge, my breathing ragged in my chest. A rasp and a wheeze.

Maybe, if I'm lucky, I made it without being seen.

I peer over the edge of the fountain, and see the Sandman still hunched over the last rag doll. I only have a second or two before he tears it apart, and comes looking for the real rag doll. *Me.*

I remove the cork from the top of the jar, the scent so dreadful that my nose puckers and I turn my face away, not wanting to breathe it in. I reach my arm over the edge of the fountain and pour the clover-green potion into the water. It makes a swirling, bubbling sound as it mixes with the already-green water, the color blending in perfectly, just as I'd hoped.

The air is briefly pungent with the scent, before it drifts away on the wind, and I place the cork back in the bottle, taking a deep breath.

Now . . . I just need to lure the Sandman across the town square. I will climb atop the edge of the fountain, wave my arms and shout, and when he races toward me, at the last, final moment, I will jump out of the way and he will plummet into the fountain. Simple as that. *Easy.*

I peek above the stone edge, looking across to the Town Hall. The Sally doll is just as I left her, resting on the steps, undisturbed. No threads snapped in half, no arms torn free.

But the Sandman is gone.

A creeping, slithering sensation inches its way down my neck. *The feeling of being watched.*

I whip around, sucking in a breath . . . and there, only a few yards away, hovering just above the ground, is the Sandman.

He's right behind me. Staring me down.

And there's nowhere to go.

My head pounds, the breath stuck at the top of my throat. *This isn't how it was supposed to go.*

His eyes are flat and dark, a wad of sand

gripped tightly in his fist. He no longer hums his lullaby, no longer tries to lull me with pleasant words. He's been searching for me, has seen through my trick, and now he's found me.

There is a sharp-edged steeliness in his gaze, a fury that won't be easily satiated; simply stealing my dreams might not be enough for him now. He will want me to suffer. He will want to tear me apart and pull out my stuffing by the clump, hearing every thread snap, every seam peel open.

I take a step back, my heels hitting the edge of the fountain.

He moves closer; slowly, cautiously. He doesn't trust me. And when he's only a foot away, he sneers down at me.

"Tricky girl," he says, his voice still a singsong, thick gray eyebrows drawing up into his forehead. "You pretend you are a rag doll, make-believe fabric and string–" He squints at me, like it's hard for him to find the words. Like he's not used to speaking in anything other than riddles and songs. "Where have you been hiding?" he asks.

He doesn't know that I went to his home in Dream Town, that I ventured through the human world—or that I'm immune to his Dream Sand. Still, I swallow and lean away from him. But he's too close now, muted white robes brushing the cobblestones, draped across him like wet curtains—and I have no way to force him into the fountain.

I had felt so certain this would work—that I could save everyone, even the human world. But the moment is slipping away. The element of surprise lost.

His eyes gleam an awful pale white, his hair sticks up from his head, ashy and wild. His beard long and wispy and tangled. I gulp down a breath, meeting the anger in his eyes. But my heart is beating like bones shaking loose from my rib cage, and my legs want to collapse beneath me.

He lifts his hand toward me, opening his palm, Dream Sand spilling between his fingers like waterfalls. He draws in a long, full breath, cheeks puffing full like moons, then he exhales in a sudden gust, like a northern wind.

I don't flinch back, I don't blink. I let the sand envelope me in a cloud, dusting my nose and cheeks and eyelashes. I breathe it in, unafraid.

And for one quick second, I wonder if my parents were wrong: perhaps the sand *will* work on me. I've spent much of my life outside of Dream Town, and maybe I'm not immune as I once might have been, and the sand will send me into a fathomless, deep sleep. Un-waking for eternity.

But as the sand falls to the ground around me, little grains sinking into the stone cracks, I blink, and look up at the Sandman. Unaffected.

Still awake.

His expression has gone slack with confusion.

"I'm not pretending to be anyone," I say to him. "I am Sally Skellington, the Pumpkin Queen." There is warmth in my chest now, heat and fury and anger. "But I was born in Dream Town." The words feel like their own conjuring, a spell, a ritual or bedtime riddle to cast things into the stars and make them true. I feel suddenly awake and alive, a woman who isn't simply a rag doll, but a ruler who has traveled to all the realms, even the human world, to set things right. Who feels a spark, a wrath growing inside her.

The Sandman's mouth turns into a deep, bewildered frown, eyes narrowed on me as if he's unsure whether this is another trick—if I might be just another fake doll, like the others. But this is no ruse.

I am the queen of this realm, and I won't let this monster take away everything I love.

Behind the Sandman, a shadow slips through the air, quick and quiet, and I stiffen my shoulders back. *Knowing.* "I'm the one queen you won't be able to put to sleep," I say to him, my mouth gone flat, thinking of the human queen I met in the library.

I suck in another breath, bracing myself.

The shadow moves closer, racing toward the Sandman.

Zero.

I told him to stay with Jack—but he came anyway. Maybe he sensed something wasn't right, that I was in danger. Maybe he's been following me all this time.

I clench my teeth, eyes trained on the Sandman. "I'm the queen who's going to stop you."

Zero closes the gap: *Ten feet, eight, three, one* . . . I pinch my eyes closed and launch myself out of the way, tumbling across the cobblestones,

feeling several threads pop at the impact, breaking apart. My leaves rise up into my nose, but I jerk
my head around just in time to see the Sandman,
his eyes gone as wide as pond stones, right before
Zero barrels into his back, and the Sandman tumbles forward . . . off-balance . . .

. . . and pitches headfirst into the fountain.

Water erupts over the side of the fountain,
like when Corpse Kid does one of his lopsided
cannonballs.

And in an instant, the Sandman disappears
into the deep, deep water.

I hold in a breath. Watching.

Waiting.

Zero races to my side, whimpering, nosing me
in the cheek. "I'm okay," I tell him, nodding. "Thank
you." *He saved me.* I lay a hand against his neck,
feeling his ghostly warmth beneath my palm,
and I'm about to let out a long, relieved exhale,
when water suddenly rises over the edge of the
fountain like a great swelling wave, crashing and

dispersing. The Sandman appears, hair and beard soaking wet, white robes now stained green.

And still awake.

The potion didn't work: it wasn't strong enough.

Maybe if I had let it steep longer, if I had added more deadly nightshade . . .

The Sandman claws toward the edge of the fountain. His eyes on me, mumbling something—a lullaby, a string of words that are unintelligible.

I gulp and scramble back, trying to push myself up but my feet keep slipping under me. Panic screams from my chest. I need to run. *But where will I go? Into the woods? To hide. For how long?*

Forever.

I manage to get to my feet, to follow Zero, who's already flitting away, about to flee past the gate and into the woods.

The Sandman's eyes flutter briefly. He mutters something else, words I can't make out.

Run, run, run, my mind yells. But something keeps me rooted to the ground: a curiosity. A feeling. And I watch as the Sandman's eyes shutter closed again and then open. *Open, closed. Open, closed.* He makes it to the edge of the fountain, arms slung over the side, trying to pull himself free. But it's no use.

The potion was strong enough after all.

Carefully, I take a step closer to him—a smile inching up at the corners of my mouth.

He tries to speak one final time, but no sound comes out, only a muttering exhale, and after one last, slow blink, he collapses against the stone edge of the fountain.

The Sandman is fully, impossibly, dead asleep.

18

The Sandman snores deeply, halfway slumped against the edge of the fountain, robes soaked with green potion water, while Zero sniffs at his white hair to be sure he's truly asleep.

Relief swells inside me like a carnival balloon, too large for my chest to contain. Zero flits back to my side, and I run my palms down his ghostly fur, then rub behind his ears. "You did good."

My insides are a mess of tangled up leaves and

nerves, wanting to cry and shout and laugh all at once. Wanting, oddly enough, to sleep.

I've put the Sandman to sleep, but I can't be sure it will break whatever sleeping spell he has cast on all the towns, and even the human world. I have stopped him, but I don't know if I have saved anyone.

I squint across the town square, and beyond the fountain, through the dazzling late morning sunlight, there is movement.

Helgamine begins to stir, her long spiked fingers wiggling, nose twitching. At the steps of the Town Hall, the Mayor rises slowly, squinting, rubbing at his eyes, then spinning his scowling face around to rub at his other set of eyes. The four vampire brothers rise to their feet, blinking at the ghastly daylight, and the Vampire Prince turns his head to one side, cracking his neck. "Vhat an awful night of sleep," he proclaims, lifting his black umbrella to shield his face from the morning sun.

"I had the worst dreams," Helgamine remarks from the other side of the town square, helping

Zeldaborn up from where she had been slumped in the doorway of their shop. "I dreamed that we lost all our warts, and that two handsome princes had fallen in love with us."

"Yuck!" Zeldaborn says. "Sounds more like a nightmare."

"But after that, I had no dreams at all," Helgamine adds, scratching at the tip of her long nose. "It was just darkness."

"I can't remember any dreams, either," Zeldaborn answers.

"Me neither," replies the Mayor, his face jerking around to show his deep scowl.

The residents of Halloween Town are stirring, but they are groggy-eyed and sore from sleeping in odd, bone-bent places. They mutter about the darkness they felt while they slept, the deep sense of falling into a bottomless black hole. "A feeling worse than death," the Wolfman remarks, scratching behind one of his ears with a paw.

The Sandman is asleep, he's no longer stealing their dreams, and now they're all waking up.

The leaves in my chest roar against my fabric

ribs, my eyes flash away from the Sandman, and I run up the street toward home, Zero right behind me. I push through the iron gate, darting up the stone steps and through the front door, letting it slam back against the wall. At the top of the spiral stairs, I find Jack in our room.

But . . . he's still asleep.

I sink down beside him, taking his hand in mine. "Jack," I say, a whisper at the back of my throat. "Wake up."

Yet he doesn't move.

"Please . . . Jack."

My hands begin to tremble. *No, no.* The others are awake. Why isn't he?

I bend over him, pressing my mouth to his. "Please," I mutter against his lips. "I don't want to be alone anymore."

And this time, I feel him stirring beneath me.

His hand squeezes mine, then his fingertips are in my long rag doll hair, and he's kissing me back.

Tears stream down my cheeks, dripping onto his bone-cold face.

"What's wrong, my wife?" he asks. "Why are

you crying?" He wipes at the tears with his fingertip, but they continue to fall onto the bed, coating the blanket like dewdrops.

"I didn't know if you'd ever wake up."

He rises slowly, still holding my hand, and leans forward at the edge of the bed. "I had the deepest sleep, but no dreams at all. And then . . ." He pauses, looking over at me. "I could hear your voice in the darkness. Calling out to me."

Zero flits around the bed, barking happily to see Jack awake, and Jack strokes his skeleton hand along Zero's white fur.

I try to wipe the tears away, but more come to take their place. "You were asleep for many days," I tell him, nearly choking on the words, and looking away to the window, remembering everything that's happened since our honeymoon, all the other realms I've seen, my time in Dream Town. *My parents*. "Something happened," I say softly. "I found a new door, beyond the Hinterland grove. And I accidentally left it open."

Jack's eyes brighten, and he drops his hand from Zero. "You found a new door? Where does it lead?"

I swallow, feeling a new ache rising up into my throat, and the loss that comes with it. "A place called Dream Town."

"How wonderful!" Jack stands up from the bed, blinking down at me.

But I shake my head. "I set loose a monster—the Sandman," I confess. "He put you all to sleep, along with everyone in the human world. He was stealing your dreams." The tears start to gather heavy against my eyelids, the fabric unable to contain them. "I was the only one still awake, so I went into Dream Town to find a way to stop him. And I—" The words shatter, slice through me. "Jack, I met my parents—they live in Dream Town. They're the governors. And I . . . I was born there. I was never built by Dr. Finkelstein at all." I swipe at my eyes, brushing away the wetness. "He kidnapped me and brought me here to Halloween Town when I was young."

Jack's mouth turns down sharply, anger rising up inside him. "He kidnapped you!" His flattened eyes cut to the doorway, like he's going to dart from our room and go in search of Dr. Finkelstein this very moment. "I never trusted him. Never liked how he treated you. But to think that he kidnapped you . . ." His expression softens a little, eyes lifting. "Take me to the doorway," he says. "I want to meet your parents. I want to know where you're from."

I shake my head and the hurt finds me again—the gut-deep pain of discovering my parents, then losing them just as quickly, still a fresh wound in my linen heart. "They were afraid the Sandman would return to their realm, so they destroyed their grove of trees. And their doorway into the human world." I let my eyes fall closed. "I can never go back there, never see my parents again."

Jack pulls me back into his arms, as if he could absorb the pain and take it from me. And I know, I would do it all over again: I would leave Dream Town and never return a thousand times just to be here with Jack, to touch his face, to feel his ice-cold lips on mine, to have a life with him in this town. To stand beside him as Pumpkin Queen.

This is the life I want. The one I'm willing to sacrifice everything for.

At last, he looks down at me. "Where is this Sandman now?"

"I put him to sleep," I say against Jack's chest. "He's in the fountain."

"You came back here alone, to stop him?"

I nod. "I had to put everything right."

Jack pulls me tighter against him, like he's afraid to let me go. "You saved us," he says.

But I shake my head. "It's my fault the Sandman put you to sleep in the first place. I left the doorway open. I let him into our town and all the others. I almost ruined everything."

"No," Jack says. "You saved Halloween Town."

He kisses me again, folding me in his arms—the place I want to stay for a thousand years. When I first discovered Dream Town, I wasn't sure where I belonged, where my true home was. But now I know. Sometimes home is a town, a house with four walls. Other times, it's two hollow eyes in a skull, a skeleton without a heartbeat. It's here—not in Dream Town or Halloween Town—but in Jack's arms.

Folded against this hollow, skeleton chest is where I belong.

I let the tears stream down my face, I let them bind us together, salt and water and fabric and bone. Woven parts of ourselves that become one.

After the moment has stretched out and become thin, Jack pulls away and says, "Take me to the tree you found."

"There's no point," I say again. "We can't travel through it."

Jack touches my nose with his fingertip and smiles. "I want to see for myself."

Back outside, a crowd has gathered around the Sandman, still asleep against the side of the stone fountain—his snore like a gale rattling windowpanes.

The Witch Sisters fuss with his clothing, as if they're considering stealing his long white robe, while Lock, Shock, and Barrel poke at his ribs with a stick. The Vampire Brothers stand in a tight circle, discussing the matter furtively, seriously; the Sandman's sleeping body is a matter to be dealt with.

I feel a sharp sense of relief, seeing the residents of Halloween Town rising to their feet after days

and days of un-dreaming slumber. I had so desperately wanted to flee Halloween Town, the
people in it, and all the obligations of being queen,
but now a new feeling stirs the leaves in my low-
est ribs—joy. It rattles through me, and I find that
I can't imagine a life without these ghouls and
ghosts and grisly townsfolk. They are my friends,
as awful as they might be. They are my family.

But before we decide what should be done with
the sleeping Sandman, Jack and I slip away from
the borders of town, away from the Sandman
and the town square, passing over the narrow
ravine bridge into the spiny woods.

When we reach the grove of trees, I lead Jack
deeper into the forest, where the crescent-moon
tree stands alone in a thicket, separate from the
circle of seven holiday trees. Vines and shrubs
are still knotted around it, threatening to grow
back over the doorway and conceal it for another
unknown number of years.

"You're from this world?" Jack asks, resting a
bony hand against the door. "A place called Dream
Town?"

Zero hovers beside me, watching Jack. I nod. "Yes."

Jack touches the doorknob, a golden color, then pulls open the door. I hold my breath, *hoping*. But inside there is only a dark, carved hole. Muted, lifeless. No drowsy wind or scent of lavender and chamomile tea swirling out from inside.

The threshold into Dream Town is long gone.

He closes the door again, and I feel the flicker of hope shrivel inside me. Grow small and tiny like a pebble.

The doorway is dead. Even Jack cannot restore what's been torn down and destroyed. The connection between two worlds shattered.

There is no way back.

I'll never see my parents again; I am a daughter lost and then found. And lost again.

"I'm sorry," Jack says when he looks back at me, his own expression sunken—like he feels the loss as deeply as I do. He folds his fingers through mine, and we walk back through the woods—the forest creaking and swaying overhead, familiar in its howling, in the late autumn chill. We leave the crescent-moon tree behind.

A worthless tree stands where a doorway once did.

We cross the bridge into the cemetery, passing the stone mausoleum where I stepped through the doorway from the human world.

Jack stops, as if a ghost or a thought has just spirited through him. "How did you know the human world was asleep?" he asks.

"I saw it."

"You went to the human world?"

"Yes." I smile a little.

Jack grins, too, impish, as though he's unsurprised by my fearlessness. "Which town?"

"I'm not sure. But there was a queen, and she was marvelous." I remember the feel of her hand beneath mine, the noble, dignified expression of her features in the portrait. "Although she was asleep," I admit. "But I imagine she is just as marvelous when she's awake."

Jack releases my hand and looks to the mausoleum, cobwebs slung in the upper corners, dead leaves clotted in the doorway. "We should go make sure."

"Make sure what?"

"That your queen is awake." He glances back at me. "Now that you put the Sandman to sleep, we should make sure the human world has woken up, too." He holds his hand out to me.

"You want me to come with you?"

His face makes an odd expression, like he's keeping a secret. "Sally, you've traveled to more realms in these last few days than I have in a year. I think you're the one who should lead the way."

I step forward, and reach out for the door. Jack and I will travel to the human world together, we will see if the queen and her people have awoken, and maybe when Halloween arrives in less than a week, I will travel with him then, too. No longer left behind on Halloween night, waiting for him to return. We will mark the holiday together. A king and his queen.

I touch the door handle—the same door I passed through only hours earlier, feeling the chill waiting on the other side. The tomb-dark air that will swallow us up. But before I can pull it wide, the door is suddenly being pushed outward, toward me.

The heavy stone grinds against the earth, a cold, entombed wind rushing out through the opening.

Zero begins to growl, as if certain another villain is about to step into our world.

I stagger back, startled, but then stop short, squinting into the dark opening as one figure appears, then another. Two people step through the mausoleum doorway, emerging into our cemetery.

I feel my mouth fall open.

Eyes unblinking.

"What is—" Jack starts, bewilderment etched into the bony lines of his forehead.

The two figures step into the sunlight, dusting themselves off, as if the journey was a perilous, untidy one.

My parents are standing before us, looking a little startled by their new surroundings, standing in a graveyard in Halloween Town. "Sally?" my mom says. Her voice teeters, then falls apart. And before I can manage a single word, she's moving toward me, drawing me into her broad, familiar arms. Her skin smelling of fresh lavender, her eyes wet at the corners.

"I don't understand," I murmur into her long, coppery hair. "I thought you destroyed the library doorway after I left."

She holds me out at arm's length, bottom lip quivering. "We convinced the others to wait," she says. "If there was a chance you could stop the Sandman, we had to give you time to try."

"We lost you once. We couldn't do it again," my father chimes in, touching my arm where it's folded around Mom. "And we realized it was wrong of us to let you go and face the Sandman alone."

"You came through the human world," I say, my eyes wide, still trying to understand, to make sense of my parents standing before me. "Was everyone still asleep?"

"No," Mom answers. "We saw a young man awake in the cemetery that we passed through to get here. It was rather difficult to avoid being seen during the day, but we managed it."

Jack steps forward, shoulders drawn back, arm outstretched. "Mr. and Mrs. Governor," he says.

"I'm Jack Skellington, Sally's husband. It's marvelous to finally meet you."

My father takes Jack's hand, shaking it wholeheartedly. "Ah, the Pumpkin King," he replies. "Good, good." But then my father's expression dips. "If you're awake, too . . . does this mean the Sandman . . . ?"

I nod. "He's asleep in the town square."

"You're sure?" Mom asks, a flicker of hopefulness in her eyes.

"Come see."

19

At the town square, everyone is still gathered around the Sandman, prodding him, arguing about what should be done.

"Everyone!" Jack announces when we approach. "These are Sally's parents, from Dream Town."

The Mayor's scowling face puckers down, all jagged teeth and pale lips. "Dream Town?" he replies. "There is no such place. What are you talking about, Jack?"

"Sally found a new tree while we were all

asleep," Jack explains, nodding toward the edge of town, and the forest beyond. "Then she and Zero put the Sandman to sleep, saving us all."

The Witch Sisters cease their tugging on the Sandman's robe, casting their eyes on me, like they're not sure I'm capable of such a thing.

"And it seems Sally is not from Halloween Town, at all," Jack continues. "She is from Dream Town."

A wave of gasps passes through the crowd. Zeldaborn faints. But Helgamine makes no move to catch her sister before she hits the ground with a sudden thump. Clown topples from his unicycle, Cyclops blinks his single eye, and Wolfman tilts his head back and lets out a strange, low howl.

Behind me, I hear the creaking of metal against the uneven cobblestones. When I turn, Dr. Finkelstein is wheeling himself away from the town square.

"Dr. Finkelstein!" Jack shouts. "Don't think you can flee so quickly. We are not done with you."

Dr. Finkelstein stops abruptly, mouth wrinkled, and peers over his shoulder at Jack, a twitchiness

in his jaw, while my parents glare back at him—
anger cut into the soft seams of both their faces.
He knows there's no escape now.

"But first," Jack says, turning his attention back
to the group, "we must decide what will be done
with the Sandman. We cannot leave him to sleep
in our fountain."

"We should burn him!" Helgamine suggests,
lifting a finger in the air.

"No, let me crush him," Behemoth interjects,
stepping forward, eyelids motionless, ax sunk in
atop his head. "Or toss him over a cliff."

There are several nods in agreement; the group
likes this idea.

"Yes, let's roll him off a cliff and watch him go
splat!" Corpse Kid adds, mouth curling into a mis-
chievous grin.

The crowd chuckles, loving the image of a flattened Sandman.

Jack takes several long, deliberate steps closer
to the Sandman, eyeing the sleeping creature.
"Now, now, we cannot simply kill him."

"We can lock him in Dr. Finkelstein's lab!"
Clown shouts from the back of the group.

Dr. Finkelstein grumbles. "I don't have room for him. He'll take up too much space."

But when Jack shoots him a look, Dr. Finkelstein snaps his mouth shut—realizing that he's in no position to argue. Not anymore. He'll be lucky if he gets to keep living in his observatory once Jack is finished with him, and isn't forced to sleep out by the swamp with the frogs.

Yet the group seems less excited about the notion of simply locking up the Sandman. They murmur and shrug; they'd prefer a more clever, grisly way to dispose of him, to ensure he never puts anyone to sleep again.

"We could make a stew out of him," Zeldaborn suggests as she gets to her feet, woken from her fainting spell. "Have a big feast at the All Hallows' Eve party."

"We're not eating him." Jack shakes his head. "He might taste awful."

The Vampire Brothers nod. "He will surely have a bitter taste," remarks the Vampire Prince.

"Please, Jack!" the Mayor implores, lifting his small hands toward Jack. "Let us decide quickly so we can move on to other things. Halloween is only a few days away. We don't have time for this."

"Yes, of course," Jack agrees, nodding and scratching at his forehead.

"Perhaps we should take a vote," the Mayor continues. "On what should be done with the Sandman. Toss him over a cliff, lock him in the observatory, or—" But the Mayor doesn't finish, because there is a stirring of bubbles in the fountain. A churning of the water.

Everyone takes a step back.

From the green surface of the fountain, two copper-yellow eyes emerge, blinking, watery. A webbed hand slaps against the edge, dripping. But it's only Undersea Gal, and she flaps her mermaid fin over the side of the low stone wall. She often likes to nap in the deepest part of the fountain, at the tippy bottom, and she must have been deep enough not to swallow the sleeping potion I poured into the soupy water. Now she slithers out onto the cobblestones. "What did I miss?" she asks, eyeing the Sandman and licking her long tongue across her fishy blue lips, as if the Sandman were something to be eaten whole.

But Jack steps in front of the Mayor. "The Sandman is the property of Dream Town. He belongs to them. They will decide what should be done, not us."

Jack nods toward my parents, and my father raises an eyebrow, glancing around the crowd of spectators, then says, "The cliff sounds reasonable to us."

The crowd cheers, hoots of excitement echoing over the rooftops. Behemoth moves toward the fountain, eager to hoist the Sandman from the water. The hum of anticipation rises. The decision is made: we will march out to the swamp cliff together and be rid of the Sandman once and for all.

Yet I wonder if this is the ending he deserves.

I pick at the frayed seam along my wrist, knowing what the Sandman did is unforgivable, cruel, and terrible, and if I hadn't stopped him, everyone would still be asleep. Yet . . . there is a trembling in my chest I can't explain.

Behemoth touches the lifeless arm of the Sandman, about to hoist him up, when there is a gurgling noise. A sputtering of breath.

Behemoth glances around, eyes doughy and confused, unsure where the sound has come from.

"He's waking up!" Helgamine exclaims, pointing her long, hooked fingertip at the Sandman.

The Sandman's eyelids twitch and jerk, his shoulders arch back. We didn't move him fast enough; the potion is already wearing off.

Someone screams, and suddenly, the vengeful crowd begins to disperse. No one wanting to stick around—to risk being put to sleep again.

Wolfman and Behemoth and Corpse Kid flee toward the cemetery. Lock, Shock, and Barrel stay a moment more, curious about the sputtering Sandman, before the Mayor ushers them away, along with Clown and Grim Reaper. The Vampire Brothers slink back into the shadows, there one moment and then gone, while the Witch Sisters scurry away to their shop, slamming the door shut. The Undersea Gal slithers up the cobblestones toward the swamp beyond town.

But Jack and I stay where we are. My parents, too. Even Zero refuses to dash away into the dark, out of sight. We watch as the Sandman begins to mutter, voice thick with sleep, trying to recite some long forgotten lullaby. His big gray-blue eyes wink open, clouded, roving around him like he's lost his sense of direction and can no longer recall where he is. But then his eyes snap firmly on me—sharp as jagged sticks broke at the ends.

I take a shivering step back.

He remembers me—the one he's been looking for all this time. And now here I am, a few short feet away. With shaking arms, he drags himself upright—moving slowly—and steps free of the fountain, white robes dripping with green fountain water. But his eyes stay settled on me, balancing himself, and I know he's going to lunge at me. He's going to try to pull me apart at the seams, leaving nothing behind, then he will make his way through Halloween Town, putting everyone back to sleep.

I stop breathing, my leaves clattering beneath my ribs.

But Jack steps toward the fountain, placing himself between me and the Sandman.

My mind begins to race, calculating how quickly I could gather more herbs and make another potion. And how we might trick him into taking it. *But there's no time left.*

Yet as I peer into the Sandman's eyes, I realize something seems . . . off. The darkness rimming his eyes is gone, the creased shadows of his features now faded. Something has changed.

I step around Jack, and the Sandman stretches his arms over his head, yawning, cracking his neck to one side then the other, clearing his throat. "So that's what sleep feels like," he moans. "How wondrous."

I flash a look to my parents, but they look just as startled. Unsure what to do.

My father steps forward, careful and cautious. "Sandman?" he says, eyes squinting.

"Ah, Albert," the Sandman replies plainly, tone easy, no longer full of sharp-tongued lullabies. "It's nice to see you. How've you been?"

"We uh–" My father stalls, scratching at his temple, then restarts, as if he's never heard the Sandman speak this way and is unsure how to respond. "You don't seem like yourself," he says at last.

The Sandman raises his thick white eyebrows.

"I don't *feel* like myself," he agrees, rubbing a hand down his long white beard, straightening it. "I feel strangely . . . rested. And—" He drops his hand, considering his words with a low slant of his eyebrows. "I think I even dreamed. I've never had my own dreams before. And it was . . . delightful."

"You put everyone to sleep in the human world," my father says, shaking his head. "And the holiday realms, too."

"Did I?" the Sandman asks, squinting, like he's trying to recall. "I was so desperate for dreams after spending all those years in the woods I guess I got a little carried away." His tone has a sheepish, almost embarrassed tinge to it. As if he has simply been caught stealing sugar cookies after bedtime, or tracking swamp mud across a clean floor.

My mother squints, eyeing the Sandman. "We had to banish you," she says curtly, no kindness in her words. "We couldn't allow you to continue stealing dreams."

The Sandman nods, little trails of sand spilling from his pockets. "I understand. But it seems . . ." He taps a finger to his temple. "I don't feel the same hunger for dreams as I used to." His eyes lift to me. "I've never slept before, never had so much as an afternoon nap." He yawns again, as if recalling all those sleepless years, centuries of putting others to sleep, but never resting himself. "But now that I have, I've seen my *own* dreams, and it was—well, it was splendid."

Jack tilts his head at the Sandman. "You could have just slept yourself," he says bluntly. "Instead of stealing other people's dreams."

The Sandman swallows, settling his shoulders. "Dream Sand doesn't work on me. None of the usual remedies will do. But you . . ." He directs his eyes back to me, piercing me with their cloud-white hue. "*You* put me to sleep." His voice catches with emotion; not anger, but something else: gratitude. "I never imagined I could have my own dreams. And now I feel . . ." He rolls his shoulders back. "I feel better than I ever have. Unusually clearheaded. Is this how everyone feels after they sleep?" His gaze flashes to my parents, then back to me.

"Sometimes," I reply carefully, still not entirely sure if we can trust him. If this isn't some trick, just like my decoys, and at any moment he will dive toward Jack, and blow what little sand he has left into Jack's face.

But his mouth sinks, and his eyes flash to the ground. "I hope you'll all forgive me for stealing your dreams." He drifts forward and holds out his hand to Jack. "No hard feelings?"

But Jack doesn't extend his hand in return. "Sally is the one who's owed an apology," he replies. "She traveled to every holiday, and even the human world, trying to find a way to stop you."

The Sandman shifts his eyes back to me, his beard draped long in front of him, a softness in his features that wasn't there before. He is not the Sandman who hunted me, who tore the fake Sally dolls apart, who likely would have done the same to me if he'd gotten the chance.

"I'm terribly sorry," he says now, voice low and remorseful. "But thank you for putting me to sleep. Having my own dreams was far more satisfying than the ones I've been stealing."

Zero hovers beside me, growling; he still doesn't like the Sandman being this close to me. But I can see from my parents' faces that he is no longer the Sandman they remember, the monster they banished from Dream Town, into the woods. He seems suddenly innocuous, harmless really, just a white-haired, white-bearded wisp of a man with sand spilling from his pockets and a dreamy look in his eyes.

Maybe he wasn't the villain of the story after all; he simply needed a long overdue nap. Like a cranky child who's had too many lemon sugar drops and gone too long without sleep.

"You can't steal any more dreams," I tell him. "Or we'll have to do far worse than banish you into a forest."

The Sandman nods, more sand spilling from his pockets, his fingertips. "As long as you'll share the recipe for that sleep tonic of yours, so I can take a nap every now and then, and have my own dreams, you have yourself a deal." His face is soft and dreamy, not the wild, cranky expression that marred his features only an hour ago.

"Deal," I say. But when I hold out my hand, the Sandman doesn't shake it; he pulls me into a firm hug, folding his arms warmly, completely around me.

20

The next day, Jack summons Dr. Finkelstein to the Town Hall—where he admits in front of everyone, even my parents, to stealing me from their home in Dream Town. "I was desperate," his mouth quivers, pinhole eyes blinking nervously. "I went into the woods many years ago, when I was much younger," he says, a tremor in each word. "I had a book in my lab about the other realms, and I had heard of something called *Dream Sand*. I . . ." His voice falls away, cracking apart, then resumes. "I simply wanted to bring some back so I could study it, perform experiments, understand what it was composed of. But when I arrived in Dream Town, I saw Sally—a real, live rag doll. I had never seen anything like her. I had tried so many times to create my own daughter, to bring her to life with needle and thread, but my experiments always failed." He shakes his head, sweat dripping down his temple. "I thought if I took Sally, and told everyone that she was *my* creation, it would prove my worth as a scientist . . . and I would finally be respected for my inventions."

Jack scowls down at Dr. Finkelstein. "And you didn't think to mention the doorway to Dream Town, that you'd uncovered a portal to an ancient realm, all those years ago?"

"I . . ." Dr. Finkelstein's eyes dart away from Jack, to his small hands clamped in his lap. "I didn't want anyone to know where Sally was really from. So I hid the doorway into Dream Town, and I never told anyone where it was." He clenches his hands together. "I gave Sally a forgetting potion of bat wings and swamp water," he admits. "She never remembered her home again."

Jack mashes his teeth together, furious, then points a long, bony finger directly at Dr. Finkelstein, and I can hear the gulp in Dr. Finkelstein's throat when he swallows, the nervous clicking at the back of his teeth. "I'm sentencing you to a hundred years of community service in Dream Town," Jack announces, voice booming across the ceiling of the Town Hall. "And you will also allow Sally unlimited access to your lab and garden, for making potions and crafting experiments, until the end of time."

Dr. Finkelstein makes a sound, like he's going to protest, but Jack sneers down at him, and he quickly snaps his mouth shut. Meekly, Dr. Finkelstein nods—maybe sensing that there is nothing he can say to change Jack's mind—then, without another word, or even a glance my way, he wheels himself out of the Town Hall, chin dipped to his chest, eyes unblinking.

My parents follow him out, all too pleased to escort him back to Dream Town, where Dr. Finkelstein will immediately begin carrying out his sentence. A hundred years of community service to make amends for what he's done. And after a hundred years, I suspect Jack might even banish him to the swamp or the screaming fields beyond town. His fury at Dr. Finkelstein won't easily be satisfied.

But *I* feel relief, to finally know the truth, once and for all. I was never Dr. Finkelstein's creation. Never stitched and sewn in the dark of his lab. I was a rag doll born in Dream Town.

And now, with the day waning, and not much time left until Halloween, Jack takes me by the hand, and we travel back into the woods, to the grove of trees. We step through each doorway, into every holiday town—to be sure the Sandman's sleeping curse has been lifted.

In St. Patrick Town, we find the stubborn, sprightly residents all awake—the leprechaun I spoke to days before still in search of his lost pot of gold in the glen, rain clouds heavy in the distance, and rainbows gleaming above the treetops.

In Valentine's Town, Queen Ruby is bustling through the streets, making sure the chocolatiers are busy crafting their confections of black velvet truffles and cherry macaroons, trying to make up for lost time, while her cupids still flock through town, wild and restless.

The rabbits have resumed painting their pastel eggs in Easter Town. The townsfolk in Fourth of July Town are testing new rainbow sparklers and fireworks that explode in the formation of a queen's crown, in honor of the Pumpkin Queen who saved them all from a life of dreamless sleep. In Thanksgiving Town, everyone is preparing for the feast in the coming season, and the elves in Christmas Town have resumed assembling presents and baking powdered-sugar gingerbread cookies.

And in Halloween Town, we have just enough time to finish preparations for the holiday: cobwebs woven together, pumpkins carved, and black tar-wax candles lit.

On the night of the All Hallows' Eve party, I sew my own black gown using the Witch Sisters' chiffon fabric, and a crown made of forged iron and dove feathers from Valentine's Town. I stand at the mirror, pressing down the silky fabric along my ribs, still feeling like myself—like a rag doll, who is also a queen. Instinctively, I tug at the thread on my wrist, but beneath the seam, I feel the softness of cotton, not the crunch of dead leaves.

When I was born, my insides were filled with air-puffed cotton—Dream Town cotton. But when Dr. Finkelstein kidnapped me, he replaced the cotton with dead leaves; he wanted no reminders of where I was really from. But now I have filled myself with both: cotton and dead leaves. Because although I am the queen of Halloween Town, I am also a daughter of Dream Town. Made of nightmares *and* dreams. A little of both.

I turn in a circle, inspecting every last stitch and thread before going to meet Jack, waiting downstairs, and I know I don't look like the Witch Sisters' vision of a queen, or as fussed over as Queen Ruby, or as regal as Queen Elizabeth II from the human world.

Because I am not like the queen of any other realm, or country.

I am Sally Skellington, Pumpkin Queen.

EPILOGUE

Jack and I wander through the woods, hand in hand.

As we near the Hinterlands, I think of how spooky and peculiar this place once felt, how hesitant I was that first time, but now it feels as familiar as anywhere else within Halloween Town. Now it is a passageway, a place that contains a doorway to my homeland.

My parents replanted their grove of trees in Dream Town, using saplings from the trees they cut down. The sprouts grew faster than I expected, for there is old magic in their roots, and within days, their grove was restored, and the doorways opened. Now our two worlds pass freely back and forth, and we just had our first All Realms Gathering, where the rulers of each world assembled in Halloween Town to discuss all manner of things affecting the holidays—like leap year and weather charts and climate change that impacts our ability to visit the human world.

The realms now work together, instead of separately.

In Halloween Town, we've even opened a Haunted Bed and Breakfast, where visitors from other holidays can come and rent a room—inspired by the cottages where Jack and I stayed during our honeymoon. The halls are filled with howling ghosts and clanking chains, which make it wonderfully impossible to sleep a wink—and Ruby vows never to stay again after only a single night.

Across the street from the bed-and-breakfast, I open a small café where residents can sip cocoa lattes, eat raspberry tarts baked in Valentine's Town, and savor orange whipped toffees that Helgamine and Zeldaborn complain get stuck in their few remaining teeth—yet they keep coming back for more. Wolfman and Behemoth sit together every afternoon sharing a pot of black rose tea, delicately holding their cups between clawed and too-large fingertips, nibbling on coconut macaroons. I even sell my sleeping tonic at the café—in a much milder dose than what I brew for the Sandman, who still stops by for a refill now and then—in scents of lavender and chamomile, herbs harvested from Dream Town.

Queen Ruby visits our town often, and we watch the sunset from a tiny café table, two queens sipping tea and eating moonlight caramels. On Valentine's Day, her cupids flutter through Halloween Town, spearing their arrows into unsuspecting residents. For a time, the Vampire Prince fell in love with Mr. Hyde, and Zeldaborn with the Mayor.

The holiday realms have become like one.

And tonight, Jack and I stroll through the spindly forest, headed to Dream Town for dinner with my parents in my childhood home, where they will surely send us home with satchels of Dream Sand and books from the Lullaby Library to read to the ghoulish children in Halloween Town to help them fall asleep.

We reach the Hinterlands but continue even deeper into the moonless forest, to the crescent tree standing alone. A tree that had been hidden for too long. A tree that holds a doorway to one of my homes.

But when Jack reaches for the door, Zero begins nosing at the thicket of vines beyond the lone tree, pulling away the bracken and moss—just as he did the day we found the crescent doorway.

I release Jack's hand, moving closer to Zero, trying to see. . . .

"There's something hidden here," I say.

Something else.

Together, Jack and I begin untangling the thicket, pulling away long dead vines and thorny shrubs. And at last, we stand back, realizing what we've uncovered.

There was never simply a single tree that led to one ancient realm.

There is an entire orchard. Hidden, tucked away. Rows and rows of magical, uncharted trees. Doorways into old, long forgotten towns.

Father Time.

Old Man Winter.

The Tooth Fairy.

Multitudes of worlds, places we never knew existed.

I smile, and Jack pulls me to him. *A queen, and her king.*

And I know, with a certainty that is knitted in my linen bones, we will spend a lifetime—Jack and I, side by side—slipping through doorways that lead to other doorways, carved into ancient, gnarled trees.

Lands to explore, adventures to be had.

But always together.

Because there is nothing quite so wasted as a life unlived. And I intend to live mine. Fully. Unbound by the rules of others. Queen or not, we all deserve these things. Freedom. Hope. A chance to find out who we really are.

Jack squeezes my hand, and smiles down at me. "Well, my queen. Where to?"

ACKNOWLEDGMENTS

This book wouldn't exist without the masterful mind of Tim Burton. Like many of you, I didn't simply watch *Tim Burton's The Nightmare Before Christmas*; I tipped headfirst into it, losing myself in the dark, shadowed corridors of Halloween Town. Also like many of you, I always felt like Sally was a character who deserved her own story. She waited a long time to tell it, but I'm so grateful to Tim and the Disney team for entrusting her tale in my hands.

I never would have dreamed this book was possible if it weren't for my editor, Elana Cohen, who had a vision for the story and dared to ask if I might be interested in writing it. Thank you Elana for going on this dark, twisty adventure with me. For all the calls to talk through plot holes and Sandman details. Forever grateful to you.

Thank you to Holly Rice for seeing the magic in this story and for carrying it across the finish line—so thankful this book found its way into your hands. Thank you Lauren Burniac for brainstorming ideas with me early on. Thank you to everyone at Disney and beyond who has worked on this book: Dale Kennedy, Sarah Huck, Emily Shartle, Manny Mederos, Soyoung Kim, Jennifer Black, Tim Retzlaff, Lyssa Hurvitz.

Thank you to my agent, Jess, for steering the ship! Thank you Kristin Dwyer for being far more than a publicist, and always making me laugh.

Thank you to Christie and Island for supplying London details and research, and for walking repeatedly through creepy cemeteries and sending back videos of catacombs while I was in the middle of writing scenes—two of the bravest people I know. Thank you Heidi Spear for your friendship and support, and for supplying art by Edward Gorey to inspire my writing—your timing is always spot-on. Thank you Adrienne Young for talking me through this wild journey. Thank you Dawn Kurtagich for your endless support and spooky aesthetic.

To my parents, thank you for loving Tim Burton stories as much as I do. For letting me watch *Tim Burton's The Nightmare Before Christmas* movie so many times on VHS when I was younger that the tape split apart and had to be repaired a few dozen times.

Sky, you're my favorite.

Readers, thank you for wandering through the grove of trees with me, for reimagining Sally with me. This story belongs to you.